Lions in the Way

Lions
in
the Way

Bella Rodman

JACKET PAINTING BY DAVID STONE

CHICAGO   *Follett Publishing Company*   NEW YORK

"I do not ask the wounded person how he feels,
I myself become the wounded person."

Song of Myself

WALT WHITMAN

Library of Congress Catalog Card Number: 66–16935

FIRST PRINTING

FOLLETT PUBLISHING COMPANY
1010 West Washington Boulevard
Chicago, Illinois   60607

T/L-5190

FOR SAMUEL J. RODMAN

Lions in the Way

A Note to the Reader

This story is fiction. The Southern border town of Jameson is non-existent. No individual (excepting those who are public figures) are meant to represent real persons. Once this is said, the author hastens to add that the story is true, and it is shaped out of the experiences of living people, young and old.

The week-long events described in this imaginary Fayette High School take place in 1959, five years after the Supreme Court outlawed racial segregation in the public schools. But the story told within the covers of this book has a past and a future, and it marks one of the many significant stages in the struggle of both Negro and white America to free itself from the great evil which was spawned on that day more than three hundred years ago when the first black slave was brought in chains to this continent.

CHAPTER ONE

SATURDAY WAS A LONG DAY for the hired help at
Tompkins' Feed and Hardware Store, but it usually went like
a breeze for sixteen-year-old Robert Jones. He had been so
busy this particular morning, however, that he had not had
one free minute for private conversation with Howie. This
Saturday morning had seemed long enough to crawl around
the world and back.

But now, the two colored employees, young Jones and his
friend Howard Carter, who was twice his age, were alone.
They were sitting on the plank floor of the loading platform,
under the wide projecting eaves. But Robby was letting the
half-hour lunch period slip away in silence. He had not
touched the paper bag containing his lunch, for his usually

11

ravenous appetite was missing. His great need this morning, urgent beyond anything else, was to talk to Howie. Yet, he found it difficult to start. His sweat-logged clothes, clinging to his muscular body, felt cooler in the shade as he drank from a pop bottle, still icy from the dispenser.

The white men were nowhere in sight, but he still found himself speechless. The pen-pushers and salesmen were in the fan-cooled, high-ceilinged office partitioned off from the rest of the store. Tompkins sold everything from twopenny nails to bales of hay. The familiar aroma—a blend of hay, grains, oils, and fertilizers—that came from the storage barns in the quadrangle facing the loading platform failed to have its usual soothing effect on Robby. Robby was taller and broader built than his companion, and although he was much younger, he shared equally in the heavy work of lifting and hauling.

"Say, you think there's gonna be lions at Fayette come Monday?" he asked with sudden intensity.

Carter swallowed the food that was pushing out his thin cheeks and burst into a loud laugh; but the laughter was turned off quickly, as if by push button when he asked, "Are you set for your party tonight? I'm gonna drop by to see how you kids behave."

Robby's question hung unanswered, and his face was suddenly blurred by a frown that quickly came and went. It was a well-proportioned face. His tightly curled hair was parted in a straight line at one side, and his clear eyes were set in broad cheekbones.

"I'm glad we decided to have that party," he said. "I

don't care who knows it, but I'm sure glad we'll be together tonight. I just don't want to be by myself. . . ."

Howie nodded vigorously. "That's natural! You don't have to apologize, boy! Monday is the biggest thing that's going to happen to you for a long time to come. There's going to be lions in the way, all right. That's one thing you can be sure of. But nobody can figure out in advance just what kind." Carter took a long swig of cold coffee from the bottle he had brought from home. "It's going to be rough," he said, his eyes somber. "Even if you don't see them, you'll think they're waiting for you. But you'll live through it."

A deep silence fell between them. It felt strange after the pent-up morning to find that there was nothing else to say, and Robby reached for his paper lunch bag with exaggerated interest. As he bit into the thick meat sandwich, he remembered the entire haunting verse that came out of Frederick Douglass' book, seeing it whole, in one complete flash of recall:

I thought I heard them say
There were lions in the way
I don't expect to stay
Much longer here
Run to Jesus, shun the danger
I don't expect to stay
Much longer here.

It was Howie who had explained the spiritual's double-talk. In Douglass' day, when a slave sang it, he was telling his fellow conspirators that he was ready to make a run for his freedom. But the others—those who saw no release from slavery except in death—sang it for earthly solace.

Howie rested his head against the brick wall after he had eaten. "When I get to your party, we'll all have a chance to talk things over," he said. "Susie has an extra job tonight, and I won't be able to stay long because I'll have to bring Donald, but I'll be there!"

Robby abandoned his vision of fleeing slaves and said quietly, almost as if he were talking to himself, "I wonder if I'll really make college and get to be a doctor." He knew it wasn't a question that came from deep inside of him, because since he was old enough to understand the full meaning of his father's death, he dreamed of nothing else but of being a doc.

"How come you worry about that right now when you got more important things on your mind? Like lions."

The boy grinned. It wasn't the first time that he had asked Howie that question, and it probably wouldn't be the last.

"Okay. You win. I guess you know that I can't stop thinking about Monday. I try to see myself walking down Main Street with the others, and I can make out the rest of the kids all right, but I just don't dig the guy up front that's supposed to be me!"

He shook his head in wonder. "It's funny how you can't see yourself or figure out what's going to happen to you no matter how hard you try."

14

"I know," said Howie, corking up the empty coffee bottle and making ready to get back to work. His strong face lit up briefly with a warm smile. "I know what you mean, but that's what makes the wheels go round. A guy can only find out who he is by what he can do. That's what growing up is all about—it goes for everybody; and it takes a while, Robby, to know yourself. But you'll get there."

CHAPTER TWO

T HE KEEN-EDGED ANXIETY, which had barely surfaced during Robby's brief conversation with Howard Carter —though their talk had nothing to do with real lions or any other jungle beasts—would have come into more tangible focus had he known that there was a stranger in town; a man whose mind was also completely concentrated on Monday morning.

Earlier that morning, twenty-nine-year-old Ben Collins and his elderly companion, Steve Prowse, stopped before the iron gate of a low fence. On the other side, a wiry, middle-aged man in washed-out blue overalls was mowing the lawn.

"Hi, Tom," Prowse yelled above the clatter of the machine. He opened the gate without waiting for an invitation, standing aside to let his important new friend enter.

Prowse handled the introduction with a proud flourish.

"Mr. Collins comes from Washington to do something for us, Tom. Just wait till you hear what he's got to say!"

They sat on the porch steps, which were out of the range of the sun, and Ben Collins entered into the business of his visit at once.

"Our friend Prowse told me you have two lovely daughters at Fayette High, Mr. Drake. I've come down here to find out just what you're going to do to stop the niggers from getting into your girls' school when it opens on Monday. I'd like to help you people if I can."

Tom Drake's eyes suddenly narrowed. "Now what in blazes does that mean! Just what do you expect *me* to do?" he exploded as his guilt-laden flush became deeper. "They made it a law in Washington, didn't they? No one wants their kids to sit next to coons, but the politicians in your lousy city got us up this tree like monkeys, and that's all there is to it!"

"Hold it, Tom," Prowse broke in soothingly. "You know not everybody in Washington is against us. Mr. Collins is getting lots of help for us up there. *They sent him here!*"

"Our friend is right," Ben added gently. He saw with quick satisfaction that the question he had put to this angry man had already served its purpose. He went on, in the same low voice, "There's a lot that can be done to save your daughters and every other white girl in this town . . . it's all a matter of organization. . . ."

17

At the thought of his daughters' menacing future, Tom's lips tightened into a thin slot before he expelled his wrath. "What a time to yak about doing something! It's been settled for months. Man, haven't you heard about the Supreme Court of the United States? Where you been? Nobody believed they'd really do this to us, but those Mount Olive niggers are going into Fayette High on Monday just as sure as you're sitting here!"

Ben had little patience with people like Drake who let things slide and then sat around moaning and blaming others, but he went on smoothly. "Even if they do get in—and I don't say that they will—it doesn't mean they've got to stay in. It's not too late to do something." He turned with abrupt cheerfulness to Steve Prowse, "We don't think it is, do we?"

Without waiting for the answer, Ben continued, "All we need is a little organization and a little guts! I think I can help you. After all, you didn't ask us to come here. I came under my own steam. Remember, it looked for a long time as though you folks could handle the situation yourselves. It's four years since the last order came from the Supreme Court, and you people held it off all this time! Our organization has problems in many places. More than we are equipped to handle. We have to pick and choose where the work can do most good." Collins' voice was blandishing, as if he were talking to an erring child.

"Let's see exactly what's going on here before we say it's all over," he went on. "It was 1954 when they ordered you to take colored kids into your school the first time—that was *five* years ago. But they didn't get in. Don't forget that!" Ben smiled triumphantly. "Then your Mayor Whitney, who calls himself a lawyer, and should know better, said he could lick the law by letting just a few of them in. He called it a token, but that's when he really buckled and his treason began to show. He lied to you and sold out. Once he gave in to those crazy nine old men in Washington, he gave every Southern traitor and subversive the green light to destroy the sovereignty of the state of Tennessee!"

Carried away by his own eloquence, Ben continued fervidly, "That was the signal for trampling the highest right of all, which is the will of the people. Then the ball started rolling. It rolled over your school board members, over the P.T.A., over the civic leaders; and it mowed down some church people like with machine-gun fire." His eyes fastened on the worried-looking Tom. "Good folks like you just let the whole thing get out of hand, Drake. But that's not the same as losing the fight. Now, is it?"

Steve Prowse stared with respectful awe at Ben Collins, deeply impressed by the newcomer's knowledge of the situation. Prowse and his wife were childless, but Steve seethed with outrage at the thought of Fayette High invaded by Negro children.

His fleshy, habitually red face was deep crimson as he broke in, "It's people like Whitney, who want to get ahead in politics, who dragged us into this. The Crestwood people don't give a hoot about our kids. They send theirs to high-priced boarding schools or a military academy where there ain't no niggers and never will be. They don't care how many mongrels are born if those blacks get into our high school!"

"Somebody," said Drake savagely, "ought to fix Whitney for double-crossing us. I could do it myself."

Ben nodded approvingly. His long talk with Prowse last night—his first evening in town—had convinced him that most of Jameson and the county were straining at the leash to reverse a surrender forced on them by the mayor's crowd. This morning, after sleeping on it, he felt confident that most of the elected officials, the lawyers, civic and business leaders, and churchmen—who had all fought so long and so hard to block the Supreme Court decision—would rally around anyone who knew how to lead them out of the capitulation.

"Collins has been sent here by important people," Prowse said, "he's got it all worked out. He's got an organization. Let the man talk to Nellie, Tom. The mothers have to be pulled into this too. When you get right down to it, you know the womenfolk just ain't going to stand for this court order crap any more than we are." Steve's face was screwed up in eagerness as he turned to Collins.

"You better show Tom that picture now," he demanded.

Ben slipped his hand into an inside breast pocket and drew out a printed sheet, which he unfolded before handing it to Drake. On it was a picture of a black man kissing a young woman whose skin appeared to be white.

Both Collins and Prowse watched Tom, who was a slow reader, move his lips as he plodded through each syllable of the meager text:

20

THIS IS WHAT WILL HAPPEN IF THE NIGGERS SIT
NEAR YOUR DAUGHTER IN FAYETTE HIGH. JOIN THE
WHITE CRUSADE TO KEEP OUR HOMES AND OUR WOMEN
AND OUR GIRLS SAFE!

When he had struggled through every word, Drake
stared at the picture a long time. The sheet of paper in his
outstretched hand trembled as he rose.

Ben announced quietly, "I have five thousand copies in
my valise at the hotel, enough for the whole county—and to
spare. We must get them distributed before Monday."

Drake nodded. "Come on in," he said through tight lips.
"I want Nellie to see this."

Before Collins followed him into the house, he glanced
at the swath of trimmed grass where the lawnmower had
begun to cut. The handlebar lay on the ground, and Tom's
garden tools were near a clump of bright zinnias. The small
garden plot and the neat white-and-gray cottage had a spick-
and-span look. The Drakes were just the kind of family people
he needed, Collins exulted. He could already see many hands
reaching out to him with their help; and he found it difficult
to believe that only yesterday he was a lone stranger in this
town.

Ben Collins had arrived at the bus terminal in Jameson
on Friday at 5 P.M. While he had stood there waiting under
the still torrid sun for the unscrambling of his baggage, he
sweated at every pore and gnawed at the thought of having
wasted valuable time because he could not afford plane fare.

21

By air it would have taken less than 120 minutes from the nation's capital to Knoxville, Tennessee; add another sixty minutes by bus to his final destination, and he still would have saved a whole day.

Time was precious to Collins. He had wasted years of it, he believed, because he was without the right backers to help him demonstrate his ability as an organizer.

His chance had come at last, and a successful operation in Jameson could skyrocket him into prominence overnight. He was in a fever to get started and grabbed up his two bags as quickly as they were dumped on the sidewalk. The weight of the larger one, which was stuffed with leaflets, pulled his right shoulder down sharply as he strode off toward Arnold's Hotel in close view of the terminal.

When the sun began to set, he had already eaten his supper and made a telephone call. In a burst of curiosity, he had even surveyed the town in a brief walk. After that, there was nothing to be done except wait. He sat on the deserted hotel veranda in a roomy straw-bottomed chair, his feet resting on the lower bar of the wooden railing. He was not a smoker, and his fingers played an incessant, silent tattoo on the locked hands resting in his lap.

The streets were almost empty in the suppertime lull before Friday night's weekend shopping. In the thickening dusk, his eyes followed the purple mountain range which almost encircled the town. City bred, Ben found it odd that it was neither country nor city, but a hybrid of both, with a bright neon-lighted Main Street stretching along the eastern flank of a four-lane secondary highway that cut Jameson in half. He was surprised to see how abruptly the commonplace single-storied frame houses stopped short where they met fields of tobacco and corn. Only the Crestwood homes on their mountain slope, nestling among the trees, showed any sign of distinction.

It was the white church spire, blurred, but still visible on the darkened slope that brought Ben's thoughts compellingly back to his immediate concern.

Arnold's, the only hotel in town, faced on Courthouse Square. Nearby stood the tall brick courthouse, the seat of local government, with its old fashioned bell tower, no longer in use. Two hundred feet away from it was Fayette High School, newly built and as handsome as any school in the United States. Collins stared at its closed windows until the bronze light of the sunset disappeared from the glass, leaving them empty and black. It made him think of this town's dangerous blindness, and he could scarcely contain his impatience as he waited for Steve Prowse to arrive. His hand restlessly fingered the notebook in his breast pocket where he had Prowse tagged as a former Klan leader, an ex-miner, born in Jameson. Prowse worked as a timekeeper now at a coal yard and was the man he counted on to provide him with information not only about local people, but about all of Henderson County, from which Fayette High School drew many of its students.

Collins remembered thankfully how he had been able at long last to win the confidence of an important congressman on Capitol Hill, who had given him Prowse's name. Without it, Ben knew, he would still be stuck in his one-room office in Washington and could not have embarked on this mission. Getting that name was like finding the key to a safe deposit box full of money. If Prowse turned out to be the right man, he thought with a lift of spirits, he could shake up this mole-like town just as if he were holding it by the scruff of the neck. The slowing down of a car in front of Arnold's put an abrupt end to his thoughts, and he jumped up as if a spring had been released in him.

Ben was on the sidewalk even before the driver had time to get out of the car. His man had arrived.

CHAPTER THREE

B Y SATURDAY AFTERNOON, Ben Collins was very
cheerful in the knowledge that he had come to Jameson with
the magic key. He was moving quickly along the chain of
contact and already installed downtown, in the home of the
Jason Abbotts on Fairfax Street.

Jason, who ran the best garage in town, was a good-
humored man in his late twenties. His rosy outlook on life
rested solidly on a steadiness of purpose in attending to business and on his reputation of being a good mechanic. He was
the proud father of an infant daughter and could afford to
give his family a home up in fashionable Crestwood, but he
was not inclined to push success. Though the Abbotts lived
near the garage, they had one foot in the hill community,

having become members of the white-spired church when its pastor, Matthew Logan, married them.

Jason's wife Cleo was a slender woman who could wear her pale blond hair unaffectedly pulled back from her face in a schoolgirl ponytail and still look beautiful. Cleo was glad to have Ben Collins as a house guest, though it was a mixed pleasure which the stranger had brought into her usually uneventful life. Collins' presence had made her realize for the first time that if the eight Negro children really got into Fayette High, the future of her own two-year-old daughter, Lila, was in jeopardy. It was unbearable to think of her child being forced someday to sit in the same classroom with colored boys and girls.

From the moment Ben's luggage was put into the spare room, Mrs. Abbott appointed herself his assistant. She made up telephone lists, called friends, and drew them into the work. With the efficiency of the time when she had been an office secretary, she put through and received phone calls for her guest. It was a revelation to watch how rapidly Ben was getting things done. The town seemed to be jumping; and as she worked, Cleo's optimism rose. She felt certain that when Tom Drake, Steve Prowse, and her capable husband got together with a man like Collins, they could be counted on to reverse the unhappy course of events, which everyone in town had been prepared to accept.

Neither Mrs. Abbott, nor anyone else in Jameson, knew that Ben's Washington establishment in which she had so much confidence, consisted of only one man, himself; generally to be found in a single-desk office on the top floor of a walkup in Ninth Street, N.W., a rundown street far from the marble halls of government in the nation's capital. On street level a small signboard that marked his "headquarters" read:

BEN COLLINS, RESEARCH ASSOCIATES, INC.

Ben was technically correct to claim that he had associates. They were his backers whose sporadic financial contributions paid the rent, telephone, heavy postage bills, and all the incidental expenses over which he had sole control. They were his collaborationists, his silent partners; too busy and too discreet to take any more active part in his work than to send him an occasional check, which could be recorded in the donor's records as a tax deductible business expense. The flow of money was not large enough to satisfy more than minimal requirements for keeping mailings and Ben going. There was never enough left over to embark on the kind of campaigns he dreamed of which would produce visible and spectacular evidence of success. Yet he held on doggedly, waiting for the chance that would take him off this treadmill; aware that either something big must come along, or instead of being lifted off, he would fall off into inglorious defeat.

With melancholy regularity, when he rebelled at the lack of progress, he would worry that he had come too late upon the scene to compete successfully with older, well-entrenched hands in the field. But he never thought seriously of turning back. Inevitably self-doubt about his chosen work only served to jog his memory of the six wasted years after he left college, which he spent as a file clerk in the Government Printing Office before finding his true calling.

In the Abbotts' kitchen, Howard Carter's wife Susie was helping Cleo prepare a late lunch for Jason and his three guests. Cleo had some fleeting doubts about the wisdom of having the colored girl in the house at this time, until she decided finally that there was little secrecy about the men's activity. Telephones were ringing in a lot of homes this Saturday afternoon where other colored maids were at work. Nellie Drake was making the telephone wires sizzle as she did her share of drumming up attendance for tomorrow evening's rally in Courthouse Square. There was also phoning going on to build up a Monday morning picket line at Fayette High. When she had thought it over, Cleo decided that it was a good thing for Susie to understand just what white people were doing about keeping the Negro kids out. Mrs. Abbott took the sandwich plate from the maid to place a sprig of parsley on it. She studied the effect of the decoration intently while trying to put her thoughts tactfully into words.

"I guess you understand, Susie, that Mr. Collins, who comes from Washington, is pretty set on stopping the colored kids from getting into our high school." She found it difficult to carry on this kind of talk with a Negro, but having started, she went on with a nervous rush, keeping her eyes averted from the woman. "I don't need to tell you that it's wrong for black and white to mix. All sensible colored folks say so, too.

I wonder you people let yourselves get pulled into such danger-ous foolishness. I honestly think it would be better for those eight boys and girls to change their minds before trouble starts. There's still time, you know."

Cleo moved briskly from the sandwich plate to examine the large tray Susie had prepared. "Some people get terribly angry and upset about race mixing," she went on, "we just don't want anything like that to happen here. I would hate to see that kind of trouble in Jameson—we aren't used to it."

The silence was long and uncomfortable for both women until Susie turned the sink faucet wide open and began to clatter dishes. Her voice accompanied the rush of water in a drawn out singsong, "Why Mis' Abbott, my boy isn't four yet. Thank the Lord I don't have to worry myself about the high school." She laughed as though the idea of her personal involvement was too comical for words.

Cleo was suddenly angry and ashamed for having been foolish enough to broach the subject. She should have known better. One just couldn't get anywhere trying to talk seriously with one of *them*. She put the sandwiches on the tray beside the iced coffee and apple pie and turned sharply upon the maid.

"All this trouble you people are making for nothing! Someone will have to pay for it! I just wish I knew who really started all this. There are people who could fix him!" This was more than she had meant to disclose, but she had lost her self-control.

Susie Carter looked up from the sink into the blazing

29

eyes of her employer, but her own were empty and her face was smooth and expressionless.

"You can take the tray in now," Mrs. Abbott said coldly. "Then see if the baby is through with her nap."

Cleo followed Susie into the summer living room, where Ben Collins was standing with his back to the bright sunlight. The floor was strewn with papers, and the men were so engrossed in their talk that they paid no attention to the food.

"That was the mistake, Abbott!" Ben Collins said, without waiting for the maid to leave. "The moment you let your pastor bring that colored choir into the church, the trouble had already started but you didn't know it. It doesn't matter that it's only during Christmas—if you give a nigger *any* rope, he's going to hang you with it. Give them an opening for mixing and before you know it, they're pushing for more. You've got to understand that."

Jason looked distressed, as though he were in some way personally responsible for the fatal error.

"Well, you know it began a long time ago," he defended himself, "before I joined the church. As I heard it, when Reverend Logan proposed the idea, he said it would be nice to have good hymn singing for the holidays. Some of those people in Crestwood are darn good talkers, and before anyone knew what was happening, there were enough votes and it got started. Our pastor may have said something about race relations then, but I really don't know." Jason's smile was uncertain. "You understand how it is, Collins, niggers would rather sing than eat, and they sure put over a hymn in a big way. . . ." His voice trailed off indecisively, because he saw the logic of Ben's argument.

"Okay," Collins said dryly, accepting the explanation as an apology. "You can see now what comes of mixing. It always figures. Logan was the *first* clergyman to support the court order after your mayor buckled. That church breakthrough was the danger sign. It's pretty bad when a minister of the gospel becomes a traitor to his own people. Pretty soon there's no one left to trust. But that's water under the dam. From now on, we keep our eye on the ball—we're holding the line in Jameson, and we can make Logan understand. You and I, Abbott, will have a talk with him right away. None of the other clergy are any problem, and he won't be if we handle him right."

Drake and Prowse, who had no contact with the church in Crestwood, listening with deep interest to this exchange, nodded assent to Ben's optimistic conclusion.

The telephone rang several times while the men ate their lunch, and Mrs. Abbott carried messages back and forth. At three o'clock, when the doorbell buzzed, she ushered in Tom's two girls, Arlene and Jenny, who were accompanied by tall, red-haired Harry Nelson, wearing a bright green shirt and tight-fitting dungarees with upturned cuffs. They were the first contingent of Fayette students to appear, and Ben's usually somber face lit up as they were introduced to him by the beaming Cleo, who had helped corral them by phone.

Collins had written in his little black book that Arlene and the Nelson boy went steady. Others arrived soon after, four boys and two more girls, and Ben shook hands with each, fixing their names carefully in his mind. Their arrival on schedule gave him gratifying proof that the links in the chain of contact were forming swiftly and neatly.

Joel Saunders came last. Nelson took him in tow possessively, pushing him toward Collins.

"He's captain of the football team. I got him to come," Harry announced loudly, proud of his achievement. "We're in the same junior class."

Collins' enthusiastic welcome was genuine as he shook the boy's hand. "Mighty glad to have you on our team," he smiled. "I wish we had more like you in this fight."

Joel's blush and his embarrassment at being singled out for extravagant welcome went unnoticed under his deep tan. He knew he wasn't entitled to the praise, because he didn't feel worked up about the "fight" the way Harry or the others seemed to be. He had come just to see what was cooking. He edged away as soon as he could, feeling more comfortable when he had slipped from under Collins' direct gaze.

Cleo eased things for the young visitors by serving iced cokes right away. Jason Abbott went off to his garage, and Drake and Prowse left the house with him, to spend the rest of the day running errands for Collins.

The time had come for Ben to take command, but inexperience made him nervous in front of his young audience. He smiled, but his dark eyes looked strained.

"My name is Ben," he said, pulling himself to full height. "I want you to call me that. You know we have an important job to do together in a hurry, and we can't stand on cere-mony." He was talking down to them, proceeding cautiously, and as he spoke, he tried to study each face separately for some clue to the effect of his words; but the ten faces became as one. He reminded himself that these boys and girls had been sent to him by their parents, and he drew courage from the thought. It meant that he had followers in Jameson and in the county, probably thousands of them. He began to talk with confidence, proud of his role as their guide and leader.

"You folks look like a fine bunch," he declared. "You look like the kind of young men and young ladies who can help save this country. Together we can defend white woman-hood against the degradation which threatens them." His eyes lingered for a moment on Arlene.

The older Drake girl was small and thin, her dark hair was stiffly waved and streaked with blond where it had been bleached; her lips were bright red; her eyebrows tweezed into a thin arch, and her eyes outlined darkly with pencil. Arlene's eyelids came down quickly under Collins' gaze, and she felt herself going hot all over thinking that Harry and the other boys were looking at her too, as they remembered the awful kissing picture which the speaker had brought into Jameson.

The wicker chairs creaked, and the young people stirred uneasily.

"Why do you think they picked on your school to let the niggers break through," Ben continued, his voice rising. "I'll tell you. They thought they could sneak it in because we got so few blacks here. They figured we were too dumb to notice before it was too late. They wouldn't try right next door in Alabama, would they?"

"Naw! They're too yellow to try it," volunteered Nelson.

"That's right. But there's another good reason. They know Jameson is not like other places in the South. That bunch in Washington has a big foot in the door here, with hundreds of their people on the payroll of the federal project in Telford, only a few miles away. Those government workers come to Main Street to spend their money and act as if they own the whole state of Tennessee. It's because of them that this is a town where a black man doesn't know enough to step aside to let a white lady pass. Where's all that going to lead to?"

"To trouble," one of the boys said.

"I see I don't have to lay it on to show you that the danger is great, and there is no time to lose. In some places in the South, black men are trying to sit next to white women in the buses. They want to sit next to them in the movies. Niggers scheme with undercover Reds and their Washington stooges to get the vote away from us and take over the government everywhere. If we understand this, we can see that our duty goes further than our responsibility to Jameson or to the South. It is the American way of life that is in danger!"

He spoke without effort, warming up for tomorrow night's rally. "We have a great duty before us," he cried. "We've got to stop this conspiracy dead in its tracks or wake up some morning to find that the niggers and the Communists have taken us over! Jameson is in the center of this fight just as the sovereign state of Tennessee has become the key to the future of our country. Your high school is the first state-supported school to let the bars down. But you and I are going to put them right up again. If we save Fayette High, we can save the rest of America from mongrelization. Is that something worth fighting for? You tell me?"

Harry Nelson jumped to his feet with a piercing Rebel yell, which the others took up gleefully. Even Saunders, upon whom the sound of Ben's voice had an hypnotic effect, found himself cheering loudly.

The noise continued until Ben, with good timing, raised his arms. "How many of you are ready to keep the niggers out of your school? Put up your hands!" he demanded.

Eleven hands flew up as Harry raised both of his. Joel's was last to go up, slower than the rest, as he decided to go along for the ride.

"Fine!" snapped Ben triumphantly. "Now you can enroll as charter members of the new Junior White Crusade, and we can get down to business." He had printed cards ready for signing. In the ceremony of bestowing membership, Collins gave each recruit an enthusiastic handclasp.

Joel Saunders let himself be carried along, not knowing and not caring where he was going. He stood in line with the others for his card. The meaning of Ben's speech had touched him lightly, but there had been the dim promise of some kind of teamwork which had its own special attraction. When he accepted the shiny white card Collins handed him, Joel looked at it carelessly. It bore a stark black cross. Under the symbol of Christ appeared the legend:

He slipped the card into his pants pocket, feeling a discomfort which he did not try to explain to himself and which he quickly brushed aside.

CHAPTER FOUR

T HE SMALL WOODEN HOUSES of Mount Olive, where nearly all of Jameson's colored population lived, were perched high on a hill overlooking the town. A wide dirt road meandered through the area, falling steeply into Main Street where the white domain began. The Negroes had to get along without sidewalks, without sewers, watermains, or a gas line. Although cheap Tennessee Valley electricity flowed right to its threshold, most families found it more within their means to use wood fires for cooking and kerosene for lamps. The shacks, naked of paint, were covered with nature's own colors—rusty tin, black tar paper, fresh bits of wood; gray, weatherbeaten siding, and swaths of shining aluminum.

Every shanty had its own outdoor privy standing close

by, looking like the spindly infant of the parent body. The hill to which Mount Olive clung was the triangular ancient roof of an abandoned coal pit. It was fenced in at one side by Jameson's garbage dump; at right angles stretched the single-track railroad which connected with the main line.

The A.M.E. Zion Church occupied the place of honor in the community, although it was built on a small patch of level ground. It stood with its dwarfed spire, like a guardsman, dominating all other buildings.

When Mrs. Louella Jones, Robby's widowed mother, left her home for her Saturday night choir practice, her son's guests had already arrived. The dance music blasted off like a firecracker while she was still within earshot. Mrs. Jones wondered if the floor would withstand tonight's goings on, but she did not look back.

The table, the chairs, and Robby's rollaway cot had been moved into his mother's room. The low-ceilinged kitchen had one door and one window; both were wide open, but the stir of a fresh night breeze could not compete with the body warmth in the crowded room. Nearly everyone was dancing. The house vibrated to the tight-reined prancing, for there was space in which to move up but nothing left over for going sideways. The unshaded electric bulb hanging from the center of the ceiling danced too; and the only framed picture on the wall, that of the heavily bearded Frederick Douglass, had jumped askew when the first couple took to the floor.

Robby Jones, his damp shirt sticking to his back, barely touched the fingers of Joyce Baker as he led her through the bouncing rhythms. His partner was the best looking and the best-dressed of all the girls. Her blue-gray eyes, set off by a coffee-and-cream complexion were bright. Her small, graceful body was tightly sheathed in a silk dress, and she wore her black, soft hair shoulder length, like a famous movie star whom she resembled.

The Baker family was rich and lived below on Jameson's Branch Street, where their ancestors had been householders for generations. Joyce's home on its run-down street was conspicuous among those of their poor white neighbors for its coat of fresh-looking paint and a flower garden. It was she who had provided the record player and the latest discs, and everyone had chipped in for the refreshments.

The Carver High School students who had been selected to go to Fayette had begun their planning of tonight's party in early spring, long before anyone dreamed of someone like Ben Collins showing up in town. But even then, no one thought of this gathering as an evening of jubilation. Without anyone saying so out loud, they knew they were getting together to build up enough steam to see them through the final hours before Monday and their plunge into the unknown. The party was planned as a strictly private affair for the three boys, Robby, Jerry, and Amos; and the five girls, Joyce, Linda, Ellen, Claudia, and Bettylou. But at the last moment, they decided to honor a few extras with invitations to make it seem like genuine hoopla.

Robby had less time for parties than anyone else in Mount Olive, and almost any girl would have suited him tonight, because he liked to dance. But Joyce had grabbed his hand when the music started. Perhaps if he had been given enough time to choose, he might have picked sixteen-year-old Linda Tilson —the tall, sturdy girl who wore her hair cut close to her head. They had both been in the same class at Carver; and like him, she was an honor student. One couldn't be in the same school with a girl like Linda and not be aware of her—she was nominated to every student office and won any post she wanted. But Robby was too busy with work and study to do more than admire her from a shy, safe distance. With his mind set on a goal that left him little opportunity to think of anything else, Robert Jones, the handsomest, most admired youth in Mount Olive, went through life innocent-eyed and oblivious to the havoc he caused in female hearts.

Linda was no exception, and her heart thumped suffocatingly when Robby was near. Even when he was out of sight, she became dreamy-eyed whenever she thought of him. As long as he danced with Joyce Baker, Linda pretended to be busy at the kitchen cupboard with preparations for refreshments. If she could not have Robby for a partner, she did not want to dance at all. She was wearing the new skirt and blouse bought especially for Monday, but she felt ugly and dressed in rags compared to Joyce, with whom no girl could compete. Rich Simon Baker's only child took upon herself the right to do things no one else dared—like grabbing Robby as though he belonged to her. It did not ease the dismal pang to know that he didn't belong to any girl; and she envied, as much as she hated, Joy's brashness.

Linda suffered the misery of her secret love until she saw Howard Carter standing in the open doorway, holding his wide-eyed son Donald on his shoulder. His arrival made her feel better at once; although it was exchanging one trouble for another. Howie brought back the remembrance of Monday with a bang as she began to edge her way to his side.

"The party just started," she shouted close to his ear.

Carter nodded and grinned, making no attempt to outshout the noise. He kept smiling because the dancers were yelling greetings without losing a beat. Linda looked affectionately at him and felt comforted just knowing that he was around. Because of him, the music must stop soon; he hadn't come only to be sociable, and he would want to leave before long to put Donald to bed.

Many of the teen-agers in Mount Olive looked upon Howard Carter as a friend. It was a compliment he earned by having helped some of them over rough spots when their own parents failed them. Under his guidance, Jerry Moore became a basketball champion, and Amos Clark began to study music seriously when Carter found someone to instruct him without pay.

There were strange stories attached to Howard Carter, told behind his back for their moral effect on the young. The gossip said that the evil one had possessed him early in life, but the Lord helped him turn on the devil and conquer him. The story varied in each telling, but few people ever mentioned that the real change took place in Howie when he went off to the Korean War.

No one remembered that until he went into the Army, Carter never read anything except the print on a deck of cards, or in the comics—the latter with difficulty. When he enlisted at twenty-four, he was aimless and chronically flat broke, with nothing better to do than be clothed and fed by Uncle Sam. He never got to Korea, but in the Army he found a Negro sergeant who changed the course of his life. When the war was over, he came back to Mount Olive, no longer the same person who had left it. He soon married his old sweetheart Susie and settled down.

It was in the Army, in endless bull sessions with the Harlem-born sergeant, that Howie had for the first time learned something about his African ancestors; about the Civil War and Reconstruction. Such knowledge made him look at himself and at the world with new eyes; and the more he learned the greater were the questions that began to plague him, demanding an answer. The sergeant's gift that Howie valued most was the ability to put the letters of the alphabet together so much more easily that he was able now to find those answers by himself. Becoming a reader was like being let out of the prison of ignorance in which he had been locked for so long.

Howie also brought back a book which his New York friend told him to buy. It was "The Life and Times of Frederick Douglass." He carried it home with the cover protected from the prying eyes of white people. He read it slowly, with painful concentration, because reading did not yet come easy to him. In Mount Olive no one except the Negro teachers at Carver High ever talked about the great Douglass. Even Reverend Jacob Wilkins, the pastor of the A.M.E. Zion Church, who was an old man, seemed to have forgotten the famous ex-slave turned statesman, until Carter came back.

When Howie finally mastered the thick book, he started to preach his own kind of gospel, mostly to the young people, and he required no tabernacle to inspire them with his new vision.

When he returned to civilian life, Carter got the job as a loader at Tompkins' Feed and Hardware Store. His wages were too low to support a wife, so Susie continued to do domestic work in Jameson. When the baby was born, she paid an elderly neighbor to care for the infant while she went out on her own job.

It was Howie who helped Robby find his first steady employment at Tompkins'. Working every weekday after school, on Saturdays and during school holidays, it was a good job for a boy who wanted to save money for college. He began by sweeping, mopping, cleaning toilets, and running errands. Later he helped with the heavy sacks in the warehouse. In the many hours the man and the boy spent side by side in work, Robert Jones became Carter's prize pupil in learning the gospel of Negro freedom.

Under the returned soldier's steady tutelage, the young people of Mount Olive found there was little difference between Howie's teaching and the Bible from which Reverend Wilkins preached; and the time arrived when the two men became joined in their common task.

"Sorry, girl," Robby told Joyce when he became aware of Howie standing in the doorway. "I've got to get the fire ready for the dogs." Without waiting for the music to stop, he squeezed through the room with Joy at his elbow, vainly pleading with him to finish out the dance. "You can help," he shouted over his shoulder as he made for the yard. He squeezed past Howie, after tickling little Donald's stomach, and got to work filling the pit (which his mother used for boiling wash) with dry kindling. While the wood blazed, he spitted the hot dogs on long sticks so quickly that Joyce could only stand by watching, her pretty face puckered up discontentedly.

When the flames died down to the right glow, Robby settled Howie and Donald near the fire in a spot that was out of line of a stampede; only then did he stick his head into the house to yell, "Time out for eats! Get it while it lasts!"

They all sat on the ground, on the sparse grass that was cool with night dew. A golden moon hung in the sky above them, as if for their private use. The food disappeared quickly, and the punch was consumed faster than Linda and Claudia could pour it. They kept the fire in the pit alive, and its blaze lit up the circle of faces around it with a rich, burnished glow. The noise was as deafening as it had been indoors, but no one could fail to hear Bettylou's scream.

"Amos Clark! Don't you dare!"

Her cry was greeted by an explosion of laughter, for no one took Claudia's loud protest seriously. Plump Amos, also known as "Fatso," was her acknowledged steady, and he let

44

himself be flattened out by the push which had accompanied the scream, falling with happy abandon right into Ellen's lap.

"That's no way to treat a lady," Robby intervened, yanking at Amos' feet. "Man!" he bellowed with make-believe anger, "You touch that woman again, and it's over my dead body."

Amos paid him back in kind, scowling as he shouted, "That boy wants every girl for himself. How come you all just sit there and let him get away with it?"

His audience chorused gleefully, "Yeah! Yeah! You go for him, Fatso!"

Amos warmed to his role. "We elected him our boss man for Fayette High, not for this party. Mister Robert Jones is no gentleman. He's a hog!"

"That's the truth," cried Pete McDonald, a Carver student who was not one of the chosen eight. "Anyway, Robby ought to keep his strength for Monday. He's going to need it. He don't play football, you know, and it might get rough down there." Pleased with his contribution to the repartee, Pete shook with laughter.

They were in the groove, and laughter swirled wildly around the circle. But it soon began to fade, then stopped abruptly. The silence which they had been keeping at bay was suddenly in their midst, and Monday morning was before them like an apparition.

"That's a dumb thing to say, Peter McDonald," Linda cried out, her eyes flashing in the dark. "It isn't muscle that's going to get us into Fayette, and you're old enough to know that." She subsided all at once, suddenly embarrassed at the thought that she was showing too much heat in defense of Robby.

"We put him in charge," Jerry Moore championed his friend, "because he's got it not only in knuckles like some guys I know, but here, too. . . ." Skinny Jerry rapped his own knobby brow.

"Come to think of it," said Amos blandly, "Robby can have all the girls, even Bettylou. I don't care if he bosses me tonight. I'm mighty glad to let him get the practice . . . you just go right ahead, man, act like you're the boss. You're President of the United States. It's okay with me. You're a black president, I trust you."

Robby smiled broadly. Monday was practically here, and it didn't seem to hurt yet. "I thank you, friend," he said with dignity, bowing his head, "I will not forget you, Mr. Clark. When the right time comes, I think I'll make you chief of garbage collection. As for you, Pete, the first thing I'll do when I'm president is fix it so you never get out of Carver." He stole a sly glance at Howie, as the abashed victim of his sarcasm was buried under the avalanche of laughter. The glow of the wood fire lit up his mock-serious face. "Come Monday," he added, "when that first promenade is over, poor McDonald won't have to worry about us anymore. And folks, he's gonna miss feeling scared."

"Sure enough!" said Pete obstinately. "How about that Collins man and the White Crusade doings I hear tell about?"

Howard Carter casually broke up the exchange. "Go easy

on Pete . . . he meant no harm. Everybody knows that since this morning Collins has been hot-footing it around trying to get some people stirred up. But we mustn't forget he's got Mayor Whitney and all the important town officials to buck up against. That bum and his friends don't have the say here. So far he is only making a loud noise, and we have to wait and see."

Howie's face lit up with a broad smile. "I was just thinking," he explained, "what can a mutt like Collins do to you that other white people haven't done already? He can only try to make it harder, but that crazy man can't stop you from doing what you just got to get done."

Carter looked down on the sleeping Donald cradled in the hollow of his crossed legs. "Mmmmh! Mmmmh! You young people sure are lucky. When I was a kid, I didn't see any hope anywhere. Nowadays you know you don't have to be cut out of your rights. It would have been easier if Collins hadn't come to Jameson, but weren't you nervous before he showed up?"

In the silence that followed, Robby imagined he saw Howie's eyes on him and was the first to speak up.

"I sure was, whenever I stopped to think about it—that's any time I wasn't asleep," he finished with a laugh.

"You weren't the only one," Carter snapped back. "So don't worry too much about that man; he isn't any more popular with the mayor than with me. Tomorrow we'll go over the whole business at church with Reverend Wilkins." He stood up to go home, holding the still sleeping Donald in his arms. "It won't be easy, but you knew that when we got started on this. And don't count on that man dropping dead before Monday. Just don't be scared—anymore than you can help."

The young people guffawed extravagantly, trying to bury Collins and the White Crusade under their mirth.

Joyce Baker pulled Robby's hand. "Come on in," she coaxed, "you owe me that dance."

CHAPTER FIVE

A FTER THE ABBOTTS and their guest had eaten
Susie Carter's company dinner of fried chicken, candied yams,
and pecan pie, Jason drove Ben Collins to Crestwood to meet
his pastor. During the short ride, he told Ben as much of
Matthew Logan's history as he knew.

Reverend Logan had received his call to Jameson during
World War II. He came from Arkansas and brought with
him a wife and the daughter and son who were now grown
and lived in the North. In his fifteen years in town, he had
become firmly entrenched and was universally liked and respected.

But Jason had not prepared Collins for the minister's
physical appearance. The middle-aged churchman was a hand-

some man, six feet tall and solidly built. It was a combination that made Ben feel dwarfed and ill at ease. Collins felt muzzled while his host made leisurely inquiry of Jason about Cleo's and the baby's health. Then he took his time filling his pipe. When he had finally achieved his first satisfactory puff, the minister acknowledged Ben's mission with well-feigned casualness.

"I understand you want to talk to me about Fayette High School, Mr. Collins. What have you in mind?"

Ben's irritation by this time left him no margin for civility.

"I've come to warn you of the serious trouble brewing here," he answered loudly, his voice out of control. "You've got to do something to head it off. Abbott says you don't like to see black and white kids mixing any more than the rest of the people in this county. You've got to prove that. If what he says is true, you can still do something to keep those eight out of the high school. I advise you to tell the people in your church tomorrow morning to keep their children out of Fayette until we get things straightened out."

Collins' arrogant demand struck Logan like a bombshell; it was the last thing he had expected to come out of this meeting which Jason had demanded only a few hours ago. He shot a questioning look at Abbott, and the eager approval he saw stamped on his face shocked him more than Collins' words.

"I don't quite see where this would lead," the minister parried, concealing his agitation. "You probably know that

Jameson tested the 1954 decision through all the courts. I'm sure you are also aware that when the supplementary directive came a year later, we interpreted it to mean that we had local jurisdiction over desegregation cases in the state courts, and we took full advantage of this. It was only after the long legal battle that we were overruled in the final appeal, and then there was nothing to do but comply with the law. If I followed your advice, what would you have us do the day after Sunday; or next week, or next month? How do you expect to alter the existence of a federal law?"

"We're going to begin at the beginning," Collins cried triumphantly, jumping to his feet. "We have an organization here, and we're taking the fight out of the hands of those who flunked their responsibility. We refuse to accept the interference of the federal court; we'll stand on the sovereign right of Tennessee to self-protection. We'll tell the people the truth—if Jameson is saved from surrender, there's a chance to save all of the South. If this town goes down the drain with the niggers, the whole South follows, and with it, all of the U.S.A. We just won't let that happen without a fight!"

"You have yet to tell me in practical terms how you can nullify the Court order," the minister countered evenly.

"I don't have to tell you what *I'm* going to do," Collins shouted down at the seated man. "I came here to tell you what the White Crusade expects *you* to do. You were the first clergyman who supported the mayor and the only minister to join his committee. We look to you to make good that mistake. The place to do it is in your own pulpit tomorrow morning!"

"I think he's right," Abbott said anxiously, visibly distressed by the turn the debate had taken. "We shouldn't give up the fight."

Logan's eyes were wide with disbelief. For the first time, he was no longer master of himself; his anger revealed in the tightening of his jaw. "That's twisting things quite a bit, Jason," he answered sharply. "You know this difficult business as well as I do. It's no secret to you that we did whatever was possible within the limits of the law to keep the Negro children out of Fayette High School." He held Abbott's worried eyes steadily as he added, "When it was all over, our final decision to submit to the Court represented the majority opinion. That decision based itself on the judgment that when we admit the eight Negroes we are handling things in a way that is least disturbing to the customs and best interests of our community."

Logan began working at his pipe, which had turned cold, realizing that nothing he had said could have had any influence on Collins; he had only tried to fulfill his duty of stopping Jason Abbott from following this stranger any further. But he remembered with a jolt that he had said nothing to refute the claim which had brought both men here. Hadn't Ben said, "I understand that you don't like the idea of mixing any more than the rest of the people in this county."

Not to offer a denial was the same as admitting that the charge was true. The minister felt unnerved at the idea of declaring himself before these two. This was not the way he had planned it. He had been waiting for years for the right moment to offer itself so that he might set the record straight. But this was not it. Resentfully he told himself that he would not be pushed into so important a step by a man like Collins.

Logan carefully placed his dead pipe on the desk and rose from the swivel chair. Jason remained seated, looking unhappily from one man to the other.

"I must inform you," Matthew Logan said coldly, addressing himself to Ben, "I am unable to support any move which seeks to interfere with the law. If this is the purpose of your visit, you have wasted your time."

"That's too bad," Collins replied caustically. "I guess it means we can't count on your help to get the others in your crowd back in line. Abbott said you have the principal of Fayette and that Barlow woman under your thumb. Well, we're not going to let that stop us from taking the ball away from you. There are enough patriotic, red-blooded men left to do what's right."

Jason stood up too, realizing that they had come to the end of the meeting. "I'm sorry you see it that way," he told his pastor. "I said to Collins I was sure that if you had a daughter going to school, you wouldn't want her to sit next to a coon, if you could help it. I brought him here because I thought you two could find a way to get together. . . ."

Jason's words affected Logan deeply. He wanted his visitors to go away quickly and leave him alone with his thoughts, which clamored to be sorted out.

Ben had the final say before they left. "It's dangerous for a clergyman to use his position for reckless interference in things that don't belong to the church," he said menacingly. "It's just asking for trouble."

When they left, the minister stood at the wide casement window opening on a garden and breathed deeply of the night fragrance, as if to clear his head. It was all too painfully evident why a member of his flock had come to him so sure of winning support for Collins.

He thought back to his younger days in his first pulpit. All of his adult life he had preached that man was created in the image of God, but because of his own sinful dissembling, never were words less purposeful in guiding men's souls toward salvation. Was it less than blasphemy to preach the divine creed while denying it in action, Matthew Logan asked himself now.

He recalled that terrible year of Negro lynchings in the Deep South and the bloody clashes up North between black and white. World War II was over, and the Nazi myth of a Nordic master race was shattered. The colored men who had fought in the U.S. Army were asking for their share of equality at home, but the only answer which white America gave was quick and brutal suppression of their revolt.

Although Jameson was untouched by the violence, Logan remembered with a flicker of pride how well he had understood the roots from which the conflict sprang. It was then that he initiated the Negro choir's visit at Christmas in his own church. The sudden pride turned quickly to guilt and self-reproach as he recalled how he had planned to go on from there to seek more vital ways of expressing his Christian duty toward his fellowmen, but somewhere along the way he had lost the direction of his conscience.

Logan turned from the window and went back to his desk. His gaze caught the neatly typed sermon ready for to-morrow's delivery, and it brought back Jason Abbott's per-plexed, unhappy face, revealing to him his own failure to do God's work. He remembered all the excuses for the failure— the opposition of his congregation; the fading away of the disturbing newspaper headlines, and the Negroes themselves seemingly giving up their struggle. Gradually, during this surface peace, the voice of conscience in him became silenced.

When the Supreme Court decision burst upon Jameson, the edict had compelled him to face himself once more. No longer did he try to forget that Christ had no favored and unfavored children. Yet he had still moved with the tide and not against it; he continued to tell himself that it was too soon to speak his mind; that it was unwise to be too far ahead of his flock and to lose their support completely. He pretended that it was enough to know that some day the Supreme Court decision would be enforced because it was a just law, guided by the will of the Lord. The truth was, he loved the praise of men more than the word of God. But today young Jason Abbott had opened a great rent in the curtain of self-deceit; necessity had finally overtaken him, and he could no longer put off declaring his real views on what Jameson called race-mixing.

Matthew Logan reached for his typed Sunday sermon and took up a pen. He began to reread it, searching out the right places for interpolations. His first task was to state clearly from the pulpit tomorrow that no one could enlist him into the camp of the White Crusade. He must condemn Collins publicly and warn the town against being drawn into a movement which would lead to lawlessness and chaos.

That much he could do at once. The sermon still left the more important question of his own real views unknown to his flock, but by the following Sunday he would have several private talks with people to prepare the ground for the next step he must take.

CHAPTER SIX

DESPITE ITS POVERTY, the A.M.E. Zion Church, of which Jacob Wilkins was pastor, carried itself with the dignity expected of a house of worship. It stood in a thin grove of small pines; its meager ground covered with crabgrass and giant burdock leaves that were white with the dust of the dry spell. But the plank threshold looked freshly scrubbed, the brass doorknobs gleamed, and the tinted glass windows were fleckless.

Mount Olive was too poor to maintain both a church building and a pastor, so every Saturday Reverend Wilkins put on a waiter's white coat at the Arnold Hotel restaurant. Here he answered to the name of "Jake" when he was summoned by a customer. Many years ago, when he was a young man and had a wife and children to support, he added to his pay as part-time minister of the gospel by working full time at Arnold's. Now that he had only himself to provide for, pay for one day's work at the hotel was enough when added to his church salary.

Mrs. Jason Abbott would have been surprised to learn how up-to-date the Negro worshipers already were on every move of Collins and the White Crusade. Her maid, Susie Carter, was not the only one to bring news to Mount Olive. The colored cooks, scrubwomen, laundresses, gardeners, handymen, nursemaids, garbage collectors, and laborers shared their lines of communication which wound in and out of white establishments.

During the recess after prayer meeting, Robby Jones stood leaning against the shady side of the church, waiting for the school conference to begin. The loud gabble of voices swirling around him were those of the Carver High School students mixed with piercing cries from the small fry, who were also caught up in the whirlpool of excitement. Robby's hands were deep in the pockets of his fresh cotton pants. His half-closed eyes gave an impression of aloofness, as if only his body was present; yet he was listening to the jumble and choosing with discrimination whatever was of importance for him to hear. Another part of Robby's mind was turned inward where it stuck hypnotically to the couplet:

> *I thought I heard them say*
> *There were lions in the way.*

The two lines followed each other endlessly like a scratched record, but the monotonous circle broke as soon as he heard Pete McDonald's voice.

"When they get through with that rally tonight in the Square, they're going to have a mob all set up for tomorrow morning. You just wait and see. My ma says she wouldn't have me go to that white school for anything, not the way things are going. She says it could end up real bad. Boy! Am I glad they left me in old Carver. . . ." He stretched the final phrase out as far as it would go, wagging his head slowly.

Robby stiffened and shifted from one foot to another.

"Pete, you know something," he said in a flat voice, "I'm glad, too, you're left behind. I don't know what we'd do if you didn't stay there and help old Jim Crow. That's the truth, boy."

The anger in him was hot as he thought that the whole McDonald family was in this with everybody else, sink or swim, even if they didn't like it, and he wouldn't let Pete get away with that kind of jazz. But even that saphead, dumb as he was, knew the difference, if you were up front in the firing line or back in the rear. It made his offense even lousier.

Pete was the only one who did not find Robby's insult funny.

"Peter McDonald!" yelled Linda above the laughter. "You're just jealous you can't go with us. Who's afraid of a cracker picket line anyway?" she said, swinging her strong-looking shoulders defiantly. She thought his mother was only a frightened bandana woman from Mississippi, but was too polite to say so; instead she flung at him, "I think you just *love* old Jim Crow!"

"Oh, yeah?"

The lame retort made even the first-graders laugh derisively.

"What's going to happen now?" Joyce Baker screamed above the din, clutching Robby's bare arm with her two hands.

Joy's bid for Robby's attention agitated Linda even more than Pete McDonald's thick-skinned meanness. She hoped fervently a miracle might still happen to keep that girl in Carver, along with the half-wit Pete. The hope was not altogether in vain, for Linda, like everyone else in Mount Olive, knew Simon Baker opposed having his daughter in school with white kids. It was only because of Mrs. Baker's notorious independence of her husband that Joyce was still one of the eight. In less than twenty-four hours, they would be walking down the hill into town; and though she knew it was wrong, Linda made a silent, passionate wish that the Lord would be kind and keep Joyce Baker from walking with them tomorrow.

"Rob—bee! You haven't answered my question," Joy persisted, "do you think that white trash is going to make a lot of trouble for us?"

Before he could pull himself together for a reply, an usher called his name from the church entrance. "Robert Jones! All of you. You're wanted inside."

He pulled his arm free. "Shucks, girl," he said teasingly, "and I was just going to tell you everything."

In the stampede for the door, he extricated himself from the crowd. Inside, he slumped heavily into the nearest empty seat. There were extra visitors from the county, who had come for the school conference, and it felt good to find himself between two strangers. The long room with its small windows of tinted glass was dimly lighted. The sudden darkness made him feel as though he were getting a moment of reprieve—though he did not know from what.

The loud buzz of conversation came to a slow halt as Reverend Wilkins began to bang a gavel on the lectern. He was an old man, tall and lean, and his face was creased with long deep lines. His iron-gray hair grew thick and close to his head, and he wore out-of-date silver-rimmed spectacles. Age had not diminished his vigor. He banged sharply until he had complete silence from the audience.

"Brothers and sisters," he intoned, "we meet at a time of greatness all around us. Strong winds of change blow through the whole world today; it is a time when the cup of glory and of sacrifice is being held to our lips. . . ."

Robby kept his eyes fixed on the speaker, thinking wryly how that wind had blown him down. Once upon a time everything had been so simple for him at Carver High; the ten-mile trip each way wasn't so bad, except for the extra fare and the bus ride which cut down his working hours at Tompkins'. But he could do his lessons on the bus. The teachers were okay, and he was a big shot there even though he didn't have time for anything but his books. The world sure had changed since that day they decided to test the Supreme

Court order in Jameson. Until then, everything seemed like a familiar, smooth road where you didn't need to look before putting your foot down. Nothing would ever be easy again, the way it used to be.

Robby's eyes sought out his mother, seated in the front row near the pulpit in a place of honor, where she was always to be found on Sunday. Since his father's death, she was a leading figure in church work. Near her were Howard Carter and his wife, with little Donald wriggling in his mother's lap.

Sitting between the two strangers, Robby was glad to be alone. He let his thoughts sink further inward, examining anew the importance of an education. Only the best education could save him from the dirty work at the bottom, which was all Negroes ever got. There was no in-between choice—a colored boy either struggled to the top or he had nothing. He was set to go for the jackpot, even though he would need not one job, but three all at once, to earn enough for college. He was willing to give up everything for medical school—sports, dating, even the smallest pleasures.

Robby felt his scalp grow tight at the thought that tomorrow all of his high-flying plans might take a nosedive. The world was a very strange place since that wind started blowing, because he couldn't figure just where it was driving him. Once before he had known the terror of facing a sudden disaster. That event was always submerged in shallow memory, and it came to the surface now without any bidding; as it always did, when an obstacle seemed to rear itself in the path of his becoming a doctor.

He was eight years old and was standing in front of the house at his mother's side moving his toes in the dust as he waved good-bye. His good-looking strong father drove off in the canvas-topped car with a cheerful look backward. By the tightening of his mother's hand he could feel her unease as she gazed after the vehicle moving down the road to go among strangers. That evening Robby stood beside his mother again. This time in the open doorway clutching her skirt as the two colored men brought the lifeless body home. There had been an accident and his father lay in the road in the burning sun until they came along. He was still conscious when they picked him up and brought him to the nearest hospital. They had made a seat of their hands gently carrying him into the cool building and they stood with their burden before the white woman at the desk. She shook her head telling them there was no place for a colored man. "Take him to Perryville," she said, "you'll find a ward for niggers there." And while she spoke he was bleeding to death from internal injuries.

He had learned when he was eight years old that there was no evading the white world, no matter how you shut yourself away from it. There was no hiding from the white man's power. With the death of his father, the security of childhood vanished forever, leaving in its place the fear of all white men.

Robby shook himself free of his thoughts and tried to

listen to Reverend Wilkins, whose voice was rising in musical singsong.

"The same Pharaohs who made the children of Israel serve with rigor," the pastor said, "who made their lives bitter with hard service, are standing in our path today, and they too will fail; and ye who are strangers in the land of Egypt today will hear the word of God, He who will bring us out of the house of bondage. We praise the Lord for giving the parents of our eight children the courage to let them walk in the thorny path trod by Jesus. But let us remember that we chose these boys and girls because they are strong enough—with our help and with the help of the Lord—to carry their cross."

As Robby heard a fervid "Amen" echoing around him, his eyes were caught by a sunbeam which seemed to hold a million dust particles. He watched the ceaseless movement curiously, studying it for the form and pattern which he felt must be there. But he soon had to give up the search, irritated by the unyielding chaos in the beam of light. Lord, he thought, I don't want to carry a cross; and he asked himself in unhappy perplexity how all this churning up of his quiet days had come about. Why did he have to go into that white school now? Why he?

The answer leaped at him at once. He remembered how great it had felt last year, when he announced to his mother that he wanted to be among those chosen for Jackson. She was pleased; and for him it was a commitment to a heroic deed. Six months later, when he was the first to be named as one of the eight, he had walked on air for days.

And it all came about because he discovered he had a history just like the white people, when Howie turned everything inside out, showing him that he had to learn about himself all over again. He had to learn it differently from the way white people wanted him to see himself. When he found out how Negroes were shortchanged and cheated out of their history, it made him mad. Until then, though the school history books had nothing of value to say about his ancestry, his teachers had filled in some of the gaps by telling about Douglass, Toussaint L'Ouverture, Denmark Vesey, and Sojourner Truth. But it was Howie, and nobody else, who put all the pieces of history together in such a way as to give it new meaning. If people don't learn from their past, Howie said, they could have no future. That was just what the white people wanted him to do—stand in the same place forever. It was an eye-opener to learn that if a boy didn't have a future to reach for, he stopped growing. Howie said, sure, go for being a doctor; *they'll* do everything to make it hard for you, but go, man, go!

When the committee selected him to be one of the eight, he was in a sweat to prove that he would not let white people cheat him anymore. He was bursting with secret pride when he heard it said publicly in Mount Olive and in town that Robert Jones was the best student at Carver, the steadiest and most respected of its youth, and therefore first to be chosen for the white high school—but the day of reckoning was still months away then.

He asked himself now, with nagging anxiety, why it was all so different today; why he was slinking from people as though he had something shameful to hide? At the sound of Collins' name from the pulpit, Robby sharply focused his attention on Reverend Wilkins.

"Things are not as bad as they look," he heard the minister saying. "Collins will be arrested tonight when he shows up in the Square. That's what Mayor Whitney promised us late last night. Mr. Sinclair of the *Courier* and the police commissioner are meeting with the mayor right now . . . they will have everything under control in the morning."

"Arresting Collins won't help any!" The sudden outcry came from Simon Baker. "It won't help peanuts," he shouted, jumping to his feet. "You've whipped up the devil's own brew I warned against. It's not your children, Jacob Wilkins, who are going to Gethsemane—they're up North, sitting pretty like the NAACP gentlemen in their fine offices. Your Communistic friend Howard Carter doesn't care either what happens. The more trouble he stirs up around here the better he likes it. We have it good in Jameson—lots better than in most places. You and your lawyers from the outside who are egging our people on better leave us in peace and let our kids go back to Carver where they belong. I'm warning you while there's still time. You just leave our kids alone! Call off your dogs!"

A chorus of horrified cries of "Shame!" "Sit down!" met the attack on the old man.

The only one to come to Baker's support was Pete McDonald's burly-looking father, who said in his slow, back-country speech that the White Crusade people were just the same old Klansmen, even if they kept their sheets on the bed. There had been no sympathy for Baker, but the nodding and muttering with which the audience followed McDonald revealed that he was striking a responsive chord. "It makes no difference," he finished ominously, "if the Klan ain't been riding here lately. It don't prove it won't."

Robby's eyes flew to the back of Howard Carter's familiar head wondering why he remained silent; but just then he heard Reverend Wilkins asking, "Did you want to say something, Sister Jones?"

Robby's mother got to her feet and faced the audience. "I didn't exactly say I did," she said with a smile, "but Reverend Wilkins reads my mind." The audience seemed to enjoy the joke with her. She went on, with a sparkle in her eyes, "I got something to say! I got to remind you that it was the good Lord who spoke through that Supreme Court. Didn't He tell in plain words that if colored children and white children are kept in separate schools, it means that they are not equal in the eyes of man? Didn't the Lord say all men are His children? We know He meant white and black and brown. It's mighty sinful to go against the Lord, and it's up to us now to save these lost white souls from hell and lead them to salvation."

Robby's gaze clung like a magnet to his mother's face. He was certain that she was talking to him only, but it seemed as though she had also succeeded in sweeping away the pall of McDonald's words.

"What's all this fire and brimstone?" she continued. "What's all this scaring ourselves like little ones in the dark?" The sound of her voice was still bantering. "I don't see anything changed much since that wicked man came here to stir up ignorant, foolish people. We know that the white folks didn't want our boys and girls in the high school until the Lord spoke to them. We colored never came by anything easy; we're used to trouble, and Jesus is going to help us through this wilderness, too. He has made the blind to see a bit of His light. You parents and your fine boys and girls who are going into that Fayette High School tomorrow morning will teach the white folks to act like Christians. Don't forget that. It's a great mission that our Savior has placed upon you—He will help us because we are doing His work."

Reverend Wilkins signaled Howard Carter to speak, even before Robby's mother had time to sit down.

Howie faced the assembly, unsmiling and somber-eyed. "Mrs. Jones reminded me of something that always gets my goat," he began. "White people act as if they own the Christian gospel; they used to sail around the world to teach it to the heathen. That's the truth, isn't it? Now they got a new gospel—and they fly around teaching the heathen about freedom and democracy. Well, they don't know much about either one. Mrs. Jones is right, we got to teach them. They'll never learn by themselves. But there's some colored folks, too, who need teaching, like Mr. Baker. He's more like a white man, because he says we just hate to have anything change around here. I guess he thinks we *like* being poor and we *like* our kids to grow up ignorant. Well, we know he's wrong because that's just what white folks say, and you know they never say anything that's the truth when they talk about us."

The audience relished the gibes and roared its appreciation, but Howie's face remained set like a stone image.

"If we listened to Mr. Baker," he continued, "there wouldn't even be that Supreme Court order which is still stuck on flypaper and won't get off nohow until we yank it off. Our kids must get the chance to prove to themselves that they were born no different from white kids. They need a fair chance at a good education; and when they grow up, they've got to get the same kind of jobs with the same wages that are now handed out to white men only. We know better than Simon Baker how colored people don't get a fair chance at anything the way things are."

"Ain't that the truth!" As the cries rang out to stamp approval on Carter's words, his sober face broke into a wide grin.

With most of the audience in the palm of his hand, Carter turned his attention to Pete's father. "As for brother McDonald's worry, I don't agree with him either—about the White Crusade being the same as the Klan. It ain't exactly the same. Things have changed a bit lately, because even the Klan knows we aren't afraid anymore to meet them toe to toe, whether they hide behind their sheets or show their naked faces. But I'm not saying we should forget about these rattlesnakes—we still got to protect ourselves against them."

Almost an hour later, when the general meeting was over,

Robby and the seven other students and their parents sat quiet and thoughtful around Carter and Reverend Wilkins for a private session. The irrepressible joker Amos forgot to bother Claudia, and even Joyce Baker, with her mother at her side, showed no sign of her usual bounce.

Robby held himself erect and attentive in his seat, his face a perfect mask of composure. This was the last chance they would have, he thought, to go over each step of the way —from Mount Olive in the morning, until all of them got back home safely. He listened earnestly to the same instructions he had heard many times before, thinking that neither Reverend Wilkins nor Howie was a fortune teller. They could plan from now till Kingdom Come, but nobody could say for sure what was going to happen tomorrow or what he would have to do.

As if Robby's thoughts had been written on his face, Carter said, "Of course we don't know in advance exactly what you're going to meet up with, but you've all been preparing a long time for something more than a picnic. But I don't want you to forget that the majority of the Fayette students voted in *favor* of your admission last term. That still works mighty strong against what Collins is trying to do."

"If that man has succeeded in his devil's work," Reverend Wilkins broke in, "if there is trouble, I pray that you boys and girls will face it with compassion for the sinners."

He took off his spectacles and polished them vigorously and put them back on before he spoke again. "But because he has come here to stir up evil, I ask each one of you to examine

70

your heart and ask yourself if you want to go back to Carver tomorrow morning instead of down there. . . ."

The sun had moved away from the windows to its noonday perch and left the church dimmer and quiet. Robby felt for the second time today that he was listening to words meant especially for him. He pulled himself more erect as he folded his arms over his chest and squared his shoulders against the back of the chair.

In the stillness, Reverend Wilkins hitched his chair forward, and a fine tracing of extra wrinkles appeared on his face as he smiled faintly. "I have a riddle for you boys and girls," he declared. "Tell me why it is that a man or a woman can sometimes stand up to their oppressors who number hundreds? Like Nat Turner or Sojourner Truth, for example? How come?" But without waiting for a reply he added, " 'One man of you shall chase a thousand! for the Lord your God, He it is that fighteth for you!' That's your answer to the riddle," he said triumphantly.

"The Bible tells us that a man must live like a man. It is his God-given nature, and when he feels the wish of the Lord in himself, even if his body is puny and weak, he becomes strong like a thousand men and is ready to do His work.

"You know how one day Nat Turner broke the chains of slavery. The time came when Nat said to himself, 'The Lord has summoned me to lead the children of Israel to freedom,' and right then he found the strength he needed to follow that call."

Under the spell of Reverend Wilkins' voice, Robby was

carried back to the old magic he knew when he was a small boy in the pastor's Sunday school. Wistfully he recalled that when he used to leave the class, he felt like a much bigger and better boy than when he came in only a single hour earlier. The memory of that wonderful feeling hurt because nothing of Nat Turner's glorious self-confidence had rubbed off on him today. He would have to go into a field of battle tomorrow without feeling strong, and he was ashamed to ask anyone if it was possible to fight both fear and the enemy at the same time and still achieve victory.

CHAPTER SEVEN

IT WAS LONG AFTER MIDNIGHT when Mary Barlow was awakened by the ringing of the telephone. Her first fearful reaction was that the sound came from one of the children, but before her feet touched the floor, she felt certain the call had something to do with the opening of her school tomorrow. She had already reached the phone in the hall, when her husband's drowsy voice called from the bedroom, "I'll get it, Mary."

Her heart was beating rapidly as she fumbled for the receiver, knowing that dentists did not usually receive middle-of-the-night phone calls from patients.

"Hello," she whispered so as not to awaken Jane and Lester, who slept with their doors open into the hall.

73

"You the teacher?" demanded a high-pitched male voice.

"Who are you?" she asked.

"Just listen to me, nigger-lover. You should of been at the rally tonight instead of shooting your dirty mouth off how you want coons to sit with white girls in school. I'm warning you to stay out of the high school tomorrow like the other teachers and keep your girl out, too. If you don't, it might be bad for both your kids. Y'hear me? It's a warning."

There was a click. The voice was gone, giving her no chance to say something against the faceless threat; no opportunity to utter a word in self-defense. It was like a sudden blow, and the attacker was gone. In that moment of shock, Mrs. Barlow became aware of Jane standing at her side in the shadowy hall, whispering, "Who was it, Mother?"

"It was a wrong number," she answered, unwilling to burden a sixteen-year-old with the truth. She put her arm around her daughter, adding, "Don't waken Lester. Go back to sleep; there's a big day ahead of us."

When the bedroom door closed behind Mary Barlow, her knees were buckling. She found her husband sitting up in bed under the light of the reading lamp, his eyes demanding an explanation. She sank into a chair facing him. Although in a daze, she tried to reconstruct the exact words of that warning. The telling did not make it less frightening.

"It must be someone who knows us," she said, tightening her lips to keep them from trembling.

Dr. Walter Barlow ran a hand over his tousled, slightly graying hair. "What scum!" he said, barely breathing the words. "There is nothing lower than the hit-and-run hero who makes anonymous threats."

"Perhaps we are taking it too seriously?" she offered the consolation, struggling against her fear. "It's probably someone who got his information about the children second or thirdhand—some drunkard who wouldn't dare do anything but threaten.

"Don't minimize it, Mary. I've been more worried than you think since Collins came into town, although I don't believe he made that call. I can tell you now I had a feeling even before he got here that the smoothness with which things seemed to be going was too good to be true. One irresponsible man can do a lot of damage sometimes . . . and our kids are an easy target; you've stuck your neck out more than anyone else in Jameson."

Dr. Barlow's worried face had a sudden, steadying effect on his wife. For his sake, she was determined not to reveal how much the call had shaken her.

"But Walter," she countered, "you've forgotten that the worst was over months ago when the names of all the colored students became public. That was the time when there should have been a reaction, if there was ever going to be one. But nothing happened. There was no sign of protest; and why should it be any different now, when the entire student council is with the administration? The majority of the boys and girls have been well prepared to accept those eight kids."

"What you say is only partly true," her husband replied calmly. "There was no public protest at the time; but I don't share any of your optimism, especially right now. It doesn't take much to stir up people's feelings about an issue like this. It's all there, right under the surface for anyone to tap who half tries. I don't want to exaggerate, Mary, but if something ugly develops, Lester may be all right, but some of the older kids could take it out on our girl. Young people are swayed by every wind that blows."

She could not deny the truth of his words. People's emotions were so easily exploited. Had not the anonymous call just frightened them both enough to cloud their reason? Walter had special cause to be disturbed. He must be remembering how his professional standing in town had been jeopardized by joining the mayor's committee. He had come through with a negligible loss of patients, but she knew the shadow of that experience hung over him tonight. Anxiously, Mrs. Barlow sought for reasons why no harm could come to Jane and Lester as she argued, "We're not living in Alabama or Mississippi! We're different. There has never been violence against colored people in Jameson as long as I can remember. Our people understand that we are not going an inch beyond what the law demands. All the work put in with the P.T.A., the radio talks, our classroom discussions, and the good work of the student council will see us through safely. You know things have a way of looking hopeless in the middle of the night." She smiled up at him. "The sky won't fall tomorrow. You'll see."

Her husband shook his head slowly. "Mary, I hate to say it at this stage of the game, but that phone call made me think of the most important factor in the whole deal which we left out—the one that can work against everything we did up till now, because that man Collins has come on the scene. Do you realize that nearly every parent in town and in the county is *against* having those colored kids in the school, in spite of all our work! Deep down in their hearts they still think it's a bad thing. Even though Collins was arrested at their poorly attended, washed-out rally, we don't know how many other vicious men who didn't get here tonight he has already set in motion—like that coward who phoned you."

The import of what Walter said struck her as so undeniably true that Mrs. Barlow's face went slack. And because she could no longer completely believe her own words, she continued stubbornly, "But the fact is, Walter, the parents did accept the school plan like law-abiding citizens. It will work out; I know it will. Time will convince you. Let's go back to sleep." And for the second time that night she added, "There's a big day ahead of us."

The late August moon filtering through the white nylon curtains bathed the bedroom in silver and in purple patches of shadow. Mrs. Barlow listened to the steady breathing of her husband and wondered if he was really asleep. Her own eyes were wide open. She could not blot out the threat against Lester and Jane. Until now she had been able to take everything with steady nerves—Collins' arrival, the horrible leaflets he had sown like poisonous seeds throughout the county; the agitation for a Monday picket line in front of Fayette—but that telephone call was different.

A warm trickle of tears rolled from the corners of her eyes. An altogether alien feeling of self-pity overwhelmed her as she thought how much she had labored to do what was right; it seemed so unjust to be punished for accepting the duty of a responsible citizen. She told herself that Walter's judgment could be wrong; there was more than one way of seeing things. It was a mark of the parents' good judgment to abide by the law despite their personal feelings. But the rebuttal did not reassure her; if Walter was correct, then all their careful preparations would fail.

How could she deny that everyone looked upon the school plan as a legal compromise? The presence of those eight black children was regarded as a necessary evil by everyone—including Walter and herself. If Walter was right, then the future was indeed uncertain because of this flaw in their plans; and it was not Collins or the White Crusade which made it so.

Mrs. Barlow felt frightfully tired, as though she had just come upon a long road still to be traveled at a time when she was too exhausted to take another step. The luminous dial on the clock told her it was two o'clock. In the morning she must ask Walter to drive Lester to school without telling the child the reason for this coddling. . . . Jane was safe with her at Fayette. They would have to meet every new situation as it arose. If they had erred, some mistakes were not irrevocable; the main thing was to recognize the truth and face it. She yearned for sleep so that she might be strong enough to face the problems which might arise in the morning.

T HE ORANGE-RED SUN was just rising over the rim of the earth when Robby opened his eyes. Wakefulness came to him instantly. He put his hands behind his head and sighed deeply as he realized that it was Monday morning.

After a night of sound sleep, he awoke with the reason for his anxiety as plain as the daylight at the window. The worry came from the thought that in some manner beyond his control he might fail to meet his responsibility. Physical hurt gave him no fear. It was the awesome thought of how many people would have their eyes on him today that was so frightening—colored people, young and old, watching from all over the United States; and worse still, the white people, waiting for him to make a wrong step.

Robby sighed again and remembered the prayer with which he had gone to bed last night. Humbly, with wide open eyes that were fixed on the low ceiling overhead, he repeated his plea to the Lord to give him the good sense to do the right thing, and the courage to see him through this single day; just enough for this one day. He did not completely believe in the efficacy of prayer, but he promised his Creator that if all went well, the next day he would behave more like a man, with a man's steadiness. He breathed deeply of the morning freshness coming in from the open window, filling his lungs with cool, clean air as if to fill his body with the strength-giving nourishment which fresh air was supposed to provide.

Robby listened for his mother's movements, but there was no sound from her room. He got out of bed noiselessly, his eyes focusing briefly on the brightly colored calendar on the opposite wall, as if he still needed to verify the date. The calendar, with its appropriate scene of golden wheat fields, said it was Monday, and that too seemed like a discovery. There was no shower or bathtub in the shack, but he was skillful at washing in a tin clothes-boiler. Last night he had taken a hot sponge bath, but this morning, after folding the rollaway cot, he just washed in cold water.

Standing over a tin basin, he sloshed water over his head and under his armpits; his thoughts pounded unchecked with the noisy sound of water in his ears. *Niggers smell niggers smell sure as anything he would hear it before the day was over dirty white crackers he would bop one of them lay him*

out flat if he heard it he would have his eyes straight ahead
and his hands at his side said the Knoxville lawyer Christ
taught us to walk in righteousness said Reverend Wilkins
walk in there like it was your right were Howie's last words
the only words that mattered.

As he straightened up and toweled briskly, his head
cleared, and he gave close attention to dressing. By the time
he was fully clothed, his mother appeared.

"Good morning, Son," she said, after a quick, approving
scrutiny. "Come help me fix breakfast."

Her voice was as comforting as the touch of a caressing
hand, and Robby started to follow her around. After the
table was set, he gave up trying to be useful and took his usual
place. Mrs. Jones put food before him and sat down, too. It
was not a breakfast for an ordinary school day but a feast—
a dish of chilled applesauce, fluffy scrambled eggs with a
slice of pink ham, homemade plum preserve, and a glass of
milk.

Robby tried to eat, but it made him gag. He looked up
appealingly. "Mom, I can't. I'm too nervous." He smiled
weakly to take the edge off the confession.

"Drink the milk," Mrs. Jones coaxed, "you'll need something to hold you until the lunch bell." Even as she said it,
her heart contracted in a spasm of pain. If he could not swallow food in his own home this morning, how would it be
in that cafeteria for this big boy of sixteen, almost a man,
eating among whites for the first time in his life . . . the food
he ate in that place would taste like dust in his mouth.

It troubled her all over again that she could not accompany him to the school grounds to see how he got in. But she had been the first to back up the NAACP lawyer who came to them from Knoxville and advised the students to walk without an escort, like normal young people, not like kindergartners. In the end, all the parents agreed; but it had been a wrench to let her son go into the unknown without her. Suppose some crazy man threw a rock and injured him permanently; maybe something worse. She hoped her fear was not visible in her eyes as she said brightly, "It's a good sign, Robby, that the Square was so empty last night. And best of all, that the mayor kept his promise and put that man Collins in jail. If there's to be some White Crusade people in front of the high school, the constables will be there, too." Louella Jones sought to reassure herself in those words, for she knew the unexpected incitement had gone on steadily all weekend.

She finally gave up any pretense of eating and sipped her hot, strong coffee; cudgeling her brain for the important thing she might have forgotten to say.

"When I come home from work tonight, Son, it will all be over. The first day is the worst; tomorrow will be a little easier." The look in Robby's eyes told here that he was not listening because he was so impatient to be first at the top of the road. "It's early, Robby, you don't need to go yet. You hear me?" She spoke rapidly now, knowing he would leave soon. "Some mean folks are going to be down there. They'll say things that will make you think the whole world is against you. It's something you'll feel even if no one raises a hand, but try to remember all the time, it isn't like that at all. Many white folks are helping us, and the Lord is always there to protect you."

"I know, Mom," said Robby, getting up to leave. "You've told me that before." He was kind enough not to say that all the stuff about white people was baloney.

"Are you afraid, Robby?" his mother asked, following him to the door.

He was much taller than she was; he smiled down at her. "I guess one minute I am, and the next, I'm not afraid of anything. But you've got no cause to worry; I can make it all right."

He had to bend down to be kissed, and Mrs. Jones restrained herself from putting her arms around him, knowing that he would not like the babying. She looked sadly into his eyes. "I know you can make it," she said. "I'm going to stay and wash up the dishes in my own kitchen this morning; this is a special day, Son."

Robby was first at the top of the hill, as he had wished it. Moments later he saw Jerry and Amos; they were talking loud enough to be heard from a distance. Four of the girls arrived in a bunch; Joyce came last with her mother, the only one to bring a parent along.

"Well, we're all here!" Jerry crowed as they clung together. You can't say Carver people don't know their own minds." He grimaced knowingly at Joyce, unconcerned that she looked at him disdainfully. "I feel like Tarzan this morning!" he cried, pounding his flat chest with both fists.

At seventeen, Jerry Moore was excessively thin and excessively tall for his age; but he was an outstanding basketball player, which in a great measure accounted for his being one of the eight this morning.

"You better watch that temper of yours when you get to feeling so powerful," Robby cautioned him jokingly. "Don't draw any fouls on us."

Linda Tilson's eyes were fixed on Joyce, whom the Lord, after all, had not seen fit to keep away from them; and as though she was being punished for her ugly unfulfilled wish, Joy Baker linked her arm through Robby's. That girl looked so stunning, even in a plain green skirt and pink sweater, that it made Linda tongue-tied with envy.

Only Reverend Wilkins' arrival ended her special misery. The gathering at the crest of the hill had rapidly grown to an unscheduled send-off. Only Howard Carter was missing, because he was already at work. The students waiting to ride the bus to Carver had left Mount Olive; but the children who went to the one-room school were out in force. Reverend Wilkins only needed to pull out his big chrome watch and young and old stared at him in quiet anticipation.

"I talked with Mayor Whitney on the phone this morning," he announced. "He told me that all the constables are on duty in front of the school. There are about two dozen pickets down at Fayette, waiting for you since dawn, but the police will keep them in hand."

Robby heard the news of the pickets calmly. But the couplet went on in his head at once:

I thought I heard them say
There were lions in the way.

He was eager to start out, but Reverend Wilkins was exasperatingly set on more talk. "There will be ugly words screamed at you," he said, "don't get upset. Keep right on walking, and you will hear nothing, and you will see nothing except the road into that school. Tonight, after supper, when we get together at the Carters' to talk over how the day went, you will be able to tell me that I was right."

At last Robby heard him announce, "It's time for you to go. God bless you all." He shook hands with each. The taut parchment skin of his lean face seemed stretched tighter than usual, and on it was the glow of tenderness visible to each of them in turn.

Mrs. Simon Baker kissed Joyce and patted her lovely soft hair into place.

It was 8:20 when the eight turned their backs on Mount Olive and walked shoulder to shoulder down the road, forming an arc which gave them the comfort of seeing into each other's face. "It's going to be a pushover," said Amos in a high squeak that betrayed his agitation. "Yeah! Yeah! But who's going to do the pushing?" he quipped.

Everyone began to talk at once to fill in the yawning pit of probability.

"I'm not afraid," said Claudia. "I mean I think I'm not afraid."

"Those pickets don't worry me a bit," Robby said coldly, evenly. "All I want is some day to get the chance to tell those

85

kids in Fayette, 'Buddy boy, I don't go for you any more than you go for me. You just let me get what's mine, and we'll call it quits.'"

"That's the wrong attitude," Joyce protested hotly. "You've got to start out feeling you can be friends."

A howl of derision came from Amos. "Sure thing, ask your new white friends to drop in and have some chitlings with you," he mimicked in a falsetto, "and see what happens."

"Just the same, it's the wrong way to start out," Joyce insisted. "You won't get them to like you that way."

The talk stopped abruptly as Main Street came into view. Robby halted, and before Linda realized what he wanted, he grabbed her hand and was saying to the others, "Get in line." They formed a column, and Amos and Jerry fell in place protectively behind the four paired girls.

It was a small, silent column. As the distance between him and Fayette began to shorten, Robby could see people near the school. He remembered that in the old days (in that dim past) when the bus took him to Carver, he used to pass Fayette and see the white kids in front of the school. He wondered fleetingly now if he could make out the sheep from the lions.

Even before he had time to abandon that vain effort, he heard a voice cry out wildly, "Here come the niggers!" His scalp prickled as he became aware of the blur of white placards waving crazily in the air. The distance between him and the cement path which he would have to walk to get to the school doors was getting very short, but his mind had shut tight against reading the pickets' signs. He heard the cry: "Niggers keep out of our school!" Each time it was as though it came from far away, from another planet; and he could not tell if there were fifty or five hundred people in his way.

When the last few feet of pavement were covered, some acute, special sense told him, without looking, that the pace of his group had remained steady. This was the important thing, he told himself. As they reached the final path to the entrance, he made a frantic attempt to see from the corner of his eye where the police were stationed, but the effort was too difficult to manage. He concentrated on navigating the last hurdle, stepping aside to let Linda and the rest of the girls proceed up the walk. A woman screamed close to his ear, "We don't want coons in our school!" He did not turn his head a hair's breadth, but watched Linda's progress toward the open doors.

He was last to walk up the path. There he saw the familiar broad-cheeked face of Joel Saunders, the white boy with the crew cut. He saw the wide grin as Joel bowed to him in mock obeisance—one hand flat on his stomach, the other outstretched—and heard him say loudly, "This way, your honor; step this way, Sir Black Baboon."

The boys and girls standing with Saunders roared their enjoyment. One yelled FIVE-SIX-SEVEN-EIGHT—WE DON'T WANNA INTEGRATE and the pack took up the cry. As he heard the chorus, Robby saw that Linda had stepped over the threshold of Fayette. Good girl, he exulted silently. We made it! Just then a woman shrieked, "My God! They got in!"

When he left the bright sun outside, everything in the entrance hall was darkly blotched, but he felt a pleasant coolness and sniffed an agreeable clean smell. As his eyes became accustomed to the indoor light, he recognized Mr. Cobb, the principal, who was looking straight at him, saying, "This way to the assembly," motioning him toward the stream of students going through wide open doors into a brilliantly lit room. There was no time to think; not even of Joel Saunders, with whom only a few days ago he had exchanged a friendly greeting on Main Street.

Robby found himself in the broad aisle of a vast auditorium that was overpowering in its splendor. Here the Negro students broke ranks, holding to their plan of mixing with the others. Amos took Bettylou and Claudia to seats. Jerry led Ellen away, Joyce followed, too bewildered to resist the arrangement. It was only when he was safely seated, with Linda at his side, that Robby was able to examine his surroundings. The beautiful glitter began to break down into separate parts as he saw the lofty, pastel-colored ceiling with its skillfully hidden lighting and a symphony of colors flowing in harmony toward the rose-colored curtain hanging across the great stage. Even the feel of the upholstered chair under him was exciting. He wanted to turn around to see if there was a balcony but was afraid of being conspicuous.

Physical contact with so much splendor was almost dizzying; it was like suddenly tasting the substance instead of the shadow of every movie he had seen in which white teen-agers rocked-and-rolled. He turned to Linda but saw with disappointment that she was staring straight ahead, her face stony, unable or unwilling to share his emotion. The bright gloss all around cracked into brittle particles as he came down to earth again, remembering Joel Saunders.

He remembered the time when Joel and he were six years old and lived near each other in Branch Street. There was always a ragged fringe of straight blond hair over Joel's eyes, because the Saunders were too poor to get him a real haircut. He and Joel shared all the leftover chicken and pie his own mother brought home from the place where she was cook. They were too young for school, but when they were together, they never needed other playmates. The thought of it astonished Robby now. He tried to fix the time when it all stopped—when and where and how—but his memory drew only a blank.

He could only think of Joel's insatiable hunger, which was just like a colored kid's; always eating if he could get food. Only a few weeks ago on a Saturday night, when they met in front of the Greek's in Main Street, Joel had said, "Hi, Robby," and went inside with his crowd to sit at a table. One of the boys wore a white T-shirt with a picture of a Confederate flag on it.

Robby was standing there with Jerry Moore when the white boys went inside, and although a moment before he had been ready to buy himself a slice of pizza pie at the takeout counter for Negroes, he suddenly just couldn't go in there. But Jerry went in and came out eating his slab of pizza.

Robby came back abruptly to his surroundings and felt the chair's smooth upholstery under his perspiring hands, but now there was no pleasure in the touch of it. The boisterousness in the assembly was an alien roar, and he felt sure there were kids in the assembly hall wearing Rebel insignia. He remembered now what had triggered his sudden distaste for pizza.

During lunch that very Saturday when he ran into Saunders, Howie proved to him that Southerners weren't joking when they talked about the damn Yankees. It wasn't for fun that there was a restaurant in the county with the name Reb Inn; and a Reb Drive-In; and a Reb Bowling Palace; and monuments all over to remind them of the past. They were still keeping the Civil War going, as if there was a chance to win back the old days—slaves and all.

That night he had eaten his bile while Jerry happily wolfed his pizza—the way *they* wanted him to—like a dog in the street. There was no use exposing his feelings to Jerry, who would only say, "You bug me, man!" and pull in his hatred for white people a notch tighter while he clowned his "yassuh" and "nossuh" into their faces. All the time he was proud as all get out that he could double-face and double-talk rings around them. But Robby didn't want to be like that nohow.

Robby's chain of thought broke abruptly as he felt Linda pressing against his shoulder and saw her frightened face.

He heard the white boy at her left spewing obscene words through the corner of his mouth as he played at being a ventriloquist. The boy's wild grimacing made him look grotesque. Robby got to his feet, conscious of the pumping of his heart, and directed Linda to change seats with him.

There was a stir and a craning of necks. A girl giggled nervously, and a boy nearby said, "Cut it out, Lang. None of that talk in here!"

Somebody was trying to save the white girls from the embarrassment of those dirty words, thought Robby, but they didn't care about Linda. Through the haze of his bitter anger, the heads that had turned in his direction had become one blurred enemy; all except the still active ventriloquist whom he saw in all his ugliness.

Lang subsided only because the curtains opened, and Mr. Cobb walked rapidly to the center of the stage. The principal was a fleshy-looking man with a round, unlined face. His dark hair was slightly gray at the temples, and he looked boyish even in middle age. He directed the assembly to stand, and his hands came down stiffly at his sides as they sang "The Star-Spangled Banner." When they were seated again, he spoke extemporaneously for a few moments; then took a folded sheaf of papers from a pocket and spread it open on the lectern.

"It is very unfortunate," he said, stopping to clear his throat nervously, "that our first day at school has been marred by the appearance of an unruly element—most of them outsiders—who seek to interfere with the orderly process of law.

I trust that these misguided men and women will quickly see the error of their ways; but just so that none of our students are influenced by the troublemakers, I shall take the precaution of reviewing some recent history." He turned his eyes to the document on the lectern and began to read.

Robby heard Mr. Cobb's slow, careful restatement of Jameson's legal struggle with the Supreme Court decision. The principal covered each step, leading up to the acceptance of the eight Negro students; and as he read on, Robby could feel the bored restlessness of the assembly. The faint hope, shadowy and feeble, that this man had it in his power to say magic words that could turn foe into friends—that hope died before he was fully aware of even having harbored it.

"If you will try to remember," Mr. Cobb cautioned when he had completed his prepared address, "that you are in school to get an education and everything else is incidental, all extracurricular activities will take their proper place while you are students here."

From the corner of his eye Robby saw the "ventriloquist" move forward in his seat to put both hands on the chair in front; the purpose became clear when he felt a weight come down heavily on his foot. The white boy looked straight at Mr. Cobb, as he held the chair for the leverage necessary to grind his heel into Robby's shoe. The Negro boy also looked straight ahead, freeing himself with a jerk and tucked his foot out of reach, far under his seat. Until the assembly was over, he sat rigid and alert, prepared for what Lang might try next.

CHAPTER NINE

WHEN MRS. JONES GOT TO HER JOB Monday, everything was topsy-turvy; the dirty breakfast dishes slipped from her hands, and a moment after putting something down or picking it up, she could not remember what she had done.

As soon as Robby had left for Fayette, she began puttering around in her own kitchen, wasteful of time, waiting for the ride into town with a neighbor. Unknown to her son, she had arranged to drive by the school to verify with her own eyes that the building which must shelter him was still solidly in its place. She was able to go on to her work then, despite her glimpse of the men and women milling around in front of the school. She saw them with their placards lowered, like standards dipped in the lull of battle.

She had turned the radio on in the Chester kitchen and was congratulating herself on how well she managed to catch the special bulletins which were coming in from Knoxville. It was a mess to be nearly two hours behind in her work on a Monday morning, but she caught each broadcast in between dusting, vacuuming, making up beds with fresh linen, collecting soiled laundry upstairs and down; emptying wastebaskets, and getting the week's wash into the machine.

She thought herself lucky to have the kind of mistress who kept out of her way. By noon Louella Jones realized that the same news was being repeated each time, the same report juggled around to appear fresh. By midday she had caught on to something more important—the broadcaster was like an actor, and the tension and the excitement in his voice was completely make believe. But just the same, each time she heard the broadcast her heart pounded with revived anxiety.

At noon he was repeating ominously: *A crowd of angry White Crusaders began gathering at dawn today in front of Fayette High to protest the admission of eight colored boys and girls. Although Ben Collins, the national segregationist leader, was arrested last night, a local command was not lacking. . . ."*

Nimbly the voice jumped from a low to a high key: *Steve Prowse, a spokesman for the Jameson organization, said that a much larger picket line would be on hand Tuesday morning. He also predicted that hundreds of his followers would be in Courthouse Square Tuesday evening for the White Crusade's second rally of the week.*

She had heard it all before, but each time the effect on her was more disturbing. Throughout the morning, while she went about her work, without willing it Mrs. Jones's memory was reaching under layer upon layer of past events she did not want to remember. She couldn't help thinking of killings and atrocities which had happened in other places.

Mrs. Jones caught herself up sharply. Jameson and those other places were as unlike as night and day. She knew how dangerous it was to open the floodgates of fear and forced herself to hold firmly to the facts—the constables were on hand as promised, and the children *did* get into the school without serious mishap. The radio would have played it up bigger than life if anyone had been hurt.

Louella Jones stopped her work, and surrounded by her mop and brushes, she clasped her hands together, thanking the Lord that it had not been any worse today. All her life she had steeled herself not to be afraid of the day to come, and Tuesday was just another day, with its own portion of hope allotted to it. The important people of Jameson were on the side of righteousness, and she would trust them to know what to do about that coming rally.

She plunged the mop into a pail of water and wrung it out to the last drop. Robby was safely past those few hate-spewing men and women she had seen on the sidewalk. There were over four hundred students in the school, and perhaps the eight colored children by now had melted away in their midst like drops of rain falling into a stream. Mrs. Jones rested her two hands on the top of the stick and smiled wanly at her own foolishness, knowing that it was no more than a vain wish. The time had not yet come for black faces to melt away easily among their white brothers. It could take a while for that glory day. She started to mop vigorously. It was a bad day for Robby any way she looked at it, and her heart ached for him. She worked steadily at her tasks, and by late afternoon everything was done. The table was set and the dinner ready, and she was ready to leave today without serving and washing up, because she wanted to be home early enough to have supper ready for her son when he got back from Tompkins'.

When she reached home, Robby was sitting in the wicker armchair, near the radio, very tired looking, his long legs stretched out. It was five o'clock, and he was back before his regular time. The rock-and-roll music blared, and on the table lay unopened school books.

"Hi, Mom," he said, competing with the radio. "Well, we got in. I'm early because I lost my job. Tompkins said I'd give his place a bad name if he kept me. He said he hated to do it. He fired Howie Carter, too." His face became overcast as he added, "We don't know how the boss found out about him." He lapsed into silence, and his face took on a look of drained emptiness.

His mother saw that it took a great effort for him to speak, but she could not deny her own pressing need.

"Shut that thing off," she demanded. "I can't hear you with that radio going." She pulled a chair up close and sat facing him. "Don't worry about the job, Son. You'll get another. Tell me how it went in the street. How was it inside?" She peered into his eyes, searching for the answer before he could speak.

Robby stirred in his chair. He had been sitting in the same spot since he got home a long time ago, but was still pooped, yet he mustered the energy to reply.

"They only yelled and made faces, Mom. The teachers and most of the kids were okay. Nearly everybody acted like we were the Thin Man—you know, just like we were glass. Some tough guy picked on us in the cafeteria, but nothing serious happened." He was too tired to tell her more; later she would have to know the rest. "Some were nice," he added, pitying the worry on her face. "The president of the student council showed me my locker and was friendly. And I'm lucky, Mom; I'm in Mrs. Barlow's homeroom, and she's my science teacher, too. I got a peek at the lab today—where we study science—it sure is something!"

"That's fine," said Mrs. Jones with a sigh, knowing that it had not been as rosy as he pictured it. He hadn't even noticed that she, too, was home earlier. "I'm pleased to hear that Mrs. Barlow is your teacher," she added. "She is a good woman."

"Linda Tilson is in my room," he added quietly. "I'm glad I'm not alone there." He stared off into space, and despite himself, now that he had spoken, Robby let slip the name which he had been trying to keep to himself, like some shameful secret. "Remember Joel Saunders? He's in my room, too."

He sagged further into his chair and closed his eyes to make it clear that he would talk no more.

Mrs. Jones rose to begin the preparation of supper. As her hand skimmed lightly over his close-cropped head, she wondered if he knew about tomorrow night's White Crusade rally.

"Some day, Son," she said, "when you're a doctor, you'll look back on this trouble and be very proud you had the strength to do what needs doing. You are going to be a fine doctor and do good in the world." She, too, fell silent, remembering that he was due at the Carters' tonight and needed some rest. When she stole a glance at the limp figure sprawled in the chair, the optimistic brave words she had just spoken seemed very hollow. While she went about getting the supper, her mind was back on a familiar treadmill: was it wrong to have encouraged him to face this trouble? Was it a mistake to wrench him out of the security of his own people at Carver? But the answer always came back the same, no matter how often she doubted. The white man gave you work, and you ate; he withheld it, and you became useless and starved or went on relief. Doctor or laborer, her boy must learn early how to live with them and hold onto his self-respect or be lost. He had chosen the difficult way to survive, but in the long run, it was the best way for him. If he was willing to pay the price, she would not stand in his way. Mrs. Jones was glad that he was to be at Howie's tonight; he was in good hands with Carter and Reverend Wilkins. They would help him.

Robby's eyes remained closed. He was pretending to be

napping, and it was almost like sleep for him to be so quiet. He had barely nodded out of politeness to the reminder that he was going to be a doctor. The idea of being a medic in a white coat was plain silly right now. That was for the birds. He couldn't see himself even a day ahead. He turned back to the question that had been occupying his mind for the last hour, the unfinished task of pinpointing the exact time when he and Joel stopped being playmates, but the answer eluded him.

All he remembered was that when Joel went into the first grade they were still together sometimes after school. But the white boy had other friends now. Then came his father's death. They had to move into the cheaper home in Mount Olive, and the separation from Joel was completed. It was not only the short, hilly road leading from Mount Olive into Jameson that kept them parted. Later he followed Joel's fortune from a distance and knew what summer jobs he took and how he became a big shot in football, with his picture in the *Courier*. Robby laughed wryly to himself, realizing how much more than the road separated them.

He lifted his eyelids cautiously to see what his mother was doing. She was wrong about the first day being the worst. It could be even more cruel tomorrow. But he felt no resentment toward her, because he knew she was trying to make it easier; and she was kind to let him off the hook when he didn't want to talk. He closed his eyes again, and the moment the lids came down Joel was standing in front of him and their eyes met. A row of grinning white kids stood like a wall at Joel's back as he bowed low and said, *"This way, Sir Black Baboon."* The others followed his example like a row of wooden puppets. Robby stood his ground and decided he would not budge until he had it out with Joel Saunders. "How come you insult me like that?" he asked. "You were once my best friend." He felt highly pleased with himself at the reasonable sound of the words. The row of puppets vanished into thin air and left them alone. But Joel looked confused and averted his eyes. Robby pushed the advantage, "I've got a right to go to Fayette as much as you. I'm an American too!"

To his amazement Joel's face became flushed and distorted with anger as he cried, "Yah! That's what you think! Fayette is our school, and you're staying out!"

Robby was speechless when he saw his mistake—there was no way to bridge the great chasm between them. By some sorcery, Joel's taunting gang was back again. This time Robby knew how to escape their jeering cries; all he had to do was to open his eyes. His eyes flew open to make certain; there was only his mother bent over the cookstove. He quickly closed his eyes again, still pretending that he was napping.

CHAPTER TEN

AT THE CARTERS' THAT NIGHT, half of the eight
young guests sat on the floor close together because there were
not enough chairs for everybody. Even without visitors, it was
a tight squeeze in their kitchen-parlor where the big white
refrigerator (a prize Mrs. Carter had won in a church raffle),
the envy of her neighbors, ate up too much floor space.

Susie Carter rested her tired feet as she sat talking with
Reverend Wilkins, all the while keeping one eye on Donald,
who fought cheerfully against being led off to bed by his
father. The little boy's playful cries became earsplitting as
Howie gave up persuasion and lifted him into his arms.

Another interested watcher was Robbie Jones, sitting on
the floor with his knees drawn up under his chin, wondering

101

what Howie was going to do about finding a new job. Branded as a troublemaker in Jameson, they could force the Carters to leave town by starving them out. It didn't make it any easier that Howie wasn't surprised. He always said colored people who showed independence found it harder to get work than anybody else. Concern over the plight of his friend mirrored Robby's own shock at being fired. Tompkins knew months ago that he was chosen to enter Fayette and said nothing about it; but now, without warning, he fired them both. Only a colored stoolie could have betrayed Howie's interest in the high school, because Tompkins was no mind reader and knew nothing about the private lives of his Negro employees. Jameson's white people knew that only Reverend Wilkins belonged to the NAACP and was Mount Olive's spokesman on all community matters.

Donald lost the unequal battle with his father and was put to bed in the adjoining room. When Carter returned and the meeting began, his eyes were bright.

"You kids were great today! And I mean *great*," he said, wagging his head, "the way you went through that pack of screaming hyenas. But something's got to be done about the dirty goings-on inside that building. Reverend Wilkins will talk to the mayor and his committee when we find out just what happened in there."

Jerry Moore needed no prompting to tell his story. "I got a bunch of nails thrown in my face in the cafeteria just as I got into the chow line," he broke out, "Joyce was right behind me and got a fistful of them in her face. Jeez! I'd like to be ready with something better than nails for those guys tomorrow!"

Robby saw Joyce suddenly hunch her shoulders. It was as though she was trying to hide from everybody, and he felt sorry for her because she couldn't take it and was acting like an ostrich burying its head in the sand.

Joyce had nothing to say. But the bitter, angry revelations came quickly without prodding from the others. With cold fury Linda told of the white boy's obscenities in the assembly. Bettylou described how a girl stuck a pin into her back while another called her dirty names.

"It was in class," she explained with trembling lips. "The teacher couldn't see anything, and when I got up to tell her, those girls acted as if I made it all up and the teacher believed them."

Amos broke in loudly, giving vent to his anger against Bettylou's tormentors as much as to his own. "When I went to my locker, just to take a look at it, I found a stinking mess there. They fixed it so I can't use it for a long time." His whole body shook as if to throw off the vile smell.

Robby withheld his own report as long as possible, for it was inexplicably difficult for him to talk about anything that had to do with Joel. An unbidden censor was at work making his speech slow to come. But by the time everyone else had spoken, he was ready with his own glib recital which he told with the proper ring of authority.

"The majority of the students didn't go for the rough stuff," he declared. "When they threw the nails at us, a crowd

103

got around and a teacher came over. Someone told her about it, even before we got the chance. She stood there and watched while we got our food. Then we divided up at different tables, and after that nobody came near us and we had no trouble." Robby stopped to smile crookedly. "We sat there for the whole lunch period, but nobody was very hungry. There was one white boy," he added smoothly, "who told one of the skunks to lay off us . . . I heard him. . . ."

Robby reported it all—everything except what was of most importance to him. He did not reveal the name of the boy who got a big bang out of calling him Sir Black Baboon, debasing him in front of those kids out in the street. Nor did he report that it was Joel who a few hours later tried to stop the goons in the cafeteria from molesting the colored kids.

Robby's clear eyes and open countenance served him well as a solid guard behind which he clutched his secret, as he tried to find the reason for Joel's shifting ideas of what was good for kicks and what wasn't. He clung to the strange fantasy that whatever was between them now had to remain theirs alone, the same as in the days when Joel and he would let no one come between them.

Howard Carter was an older hand than Robby at hiding his feelings, but his face was grim when he heard what the young people had to say.

"Mayor Whitney must stop this stuff," he said without wasting words to assuage their hurt. "I've got to tell you that tomorrow may not be any easier because Collins is behind those kids, and he was let out of jail at five o'clock this afternoon. He's still hanging around here. But if we hold on, it will be okay. They're really trying to run him out, because the mayor wants his school plan to go through peacefully as much as we do. It's their plan, not ours, and he's going to do what he thinks is right to make it work. He made a mistake when he used the law about breaking a local ordinance for the arrest. They couldn't hold Collins in the can with that one." Howie's face broke into a smile that did not match the absence of humor in his eyes. "You know how careful they are about the law being just the right one when a white bum goes into the lockup."

As the appreciative hooting that met his sarcasm subsided, Carter's eyes settled on Jerry Moore.

"We can count on the police keeping things under control outside tomorrow morning," he continued, "but you people need to be prepared to take anything those kids do inside the building. You'll just have to take it until Reverend Wilkins makes Whitney and the principal understand what's going on in there. Until then, I hope nobody in this room is going to carry more than a handkerchief in his pocket tomorrow. A clean one, please, folks."

Jerry Moore looked abashed. "I was only kidding," he protested loudly.

"I know you were, boy. But a reminder can't hurt. This was a rough day for all of you; but you did fine, and it was a breakthrough, as we say in the Army. You know war is hell. Now you can move forward, if you keep up the push. Our friend Robby got the worst of it, because they know he's the leader. That's why he lost his job today. Tompkins and his gang figure that's enough to make him go back to Carver, with the rest of you caving in with him."

"Nuts to Tompkins," cried Jerry. "We can take it as fast as they dish it out."

"That Tompkins is a fool," Linda said firmly, "if that's what he expects. Others have made it all by themselves. What makes him crazy enough to think eight of us can't?"

Robby looked hard at Linda as she spoke, wondering at her confidence. He believed Jerry's denial, because only a hophead would take any kind of a weapon into that high school after all the instructions they were given about not hitting back under any circumstances. But both Jerry and Linda were way out if they thought everybody could take all the stuff that was being dumped on them. He wasn't taking bets on anybody's self-control tonight, not even on his own.

Reverend Wilkins did not let the gathering break up until he had offered a prayer and beseeched the Lord's protection for the eight boys and girls. Robby Jones kept his head lowered during prayer and was thinking how unbelievable it seemed that he, Robert Jones, was really trying to go against all of white Jameson; planning the sort of life for himself which they said was never meant for colored boys.

CHAPTER ELEVEN

I

T WAS OLD-FASHIONED to have green plants in a classroom, but the Boston fern (a gift from pupils already out in the world) always had its sunny place in Mrs. Barlow's homeroom, and year after year its graceful fronds grew larger and more beautiful. As she stood facing the students on Tuesday morning, her eyes rested briefly on the flourishing plant, and it was a welcome source of comfort, reminding her of those satisfying years of teaching.

Little real work had been accomplished yesterday, and at this early hour, hostile men and women were again in front of the school; the stranger Collins was prominently in the forefront. The ranks of the White Crusade had increased by no more than another dozen overnight, but the teacher felt their baneful influence even more than on the first day. The six overage policemen on the town force, who generally had little to do except control out-of-town traffic, kept the demonstrators on the far side of the road, but the noisy pickets unnerved her. Just when she thought peace had come and they were gone, the abrasive shouting began all over again.

Mrs. Barlow had learned Monday morning that she was the only teacher to have received a threatening phone call. The knowledge that she was so singularly marked by the White Crusade had since then slowly nibbled away at her poise. Almost in self-defense, she brooded over the fact that leadership had not been of her own seeking. It was thrust upon her when the rest of the faculty sat back and watched as she took over the main responsibility for advancing the mayor's plan. There had been penalties to suffer when she began to advocate the unpopular cause. The worst had been the alienation of old friends and neighbors and the danger to her husband's career. But nothing had affected her as deeply as that Sunday night telephone call. Until then she had not known such murderous, crazy hate existed in the world.

A sudden explosion of shouting from the outside set her teeth on edge, and she glanced furtively at the expressionless face of Robby Jones and then at the equally inscrutable Linda Tilson, sitting in a different part of the room. It was a hot morning, but she brusquely asked a monitor to close all the windows. The paper from which she was preparing to read trembled in her hand, and she put it down on the desk to hide the telltale nervousness.

As the muffled noise from the street rose again, she could not stop herself from looking at the Negro boy and girl a second time, wondering how the courage came to them to sit there so quietly, so controlled. It came as a revelation to discover that until now she not aware that even if everything had gone through peacefully as planned, the Negro children would still need enormous strength of character to venture into Fayette. They were the rejected outsiders, outnumbered and stamped as inferiors by all the children who surrounded them. At this moment Mrs. Barlow could almost touch the invisible wall separating the colored boy and girl from the others; its invisibility made their exile no less real.

"In view of the disturbance outside," she announced in a deceptively firm voice, "the notice I have here from Mr. Cobb should be of interest to you. As most of you already know, that man Collins, who calls himself a leader of the White Crusade, was released from jail yesterday. Last night he went with friends of his to Mr. Cobb's home and ordered him to expel the eight Negro students or resign as principal of our school."

Mrs. Barlow saw the redheaded Nelson boy turn a knowing smile on a girl seated near him and heard his rude "Yassum!" but she ignored the interruption.

"Since we had close to one hundred per cent attendance yesterday, we can rightfully ask where those people got the authority to demand this. The principal is acting under a court order. We all know that was how matters stood before summer vacation. But last night Mr. Cobb made the very generous offer to resign any time a majority of the parents and students say they are ready to become lawbreakers. He wants to take a vote today to put a quick stop to Collins' agitation."

Harry Nelson shuffled his feet noisily, as he held his hand up high.

"You will have the opportunity to make your views known when I am through speaking," the teacher said crisply.

"All Fayette students," she continued, "will cast their votes in school today and take ballots home to their parents. These are to be returned tomorrow morning. There hasn't been time to prepare the forms, but we can make our own."

"I don't think we should waste time on that stuff," Nelson interrupted. "We jawed plenty about it last term. We come to school to be educated and not to waste a lot of time. This is a free country, and I don't have to go to school with niggers if I don't want to."

Mrs. Barlow saw a hand jump into the air, and she nodded, giving Andrew Sinclair, who was editor of the *Fayette Trumpet,* permission to speak.

"I don't call it freedom to go against the law and to make your own rules," Andrew said hotly. "I just don't see how anyone can object to voting. We ought to be glad Mr. Cobb made that offer. This trouble is something new and kind of suspicious the way it started up so suddenly. The parents and the students had their chance last term to say what they thought about the whole thing, and it was all settled. That is, we thought it was," he added with heavy sarcasm. "I say a vote now would show those people they're way off beam."

110

There was a chorus of approval as Sinclair finished, and for the first time this morning a little of the gloom lifted from Mrs. Barlow. Young Sinclair was not an average student. His father was publisher of the weekly *Jameson Courier* which supported the mayor's position, so Andrew's views did not surprise her. But the response of the others was something to cheer her.

"I think it is fair to say," she declared, "that we can now go on with the vote, which has two propositions. We will distribute two sheets of paper for each student on which you will copy what I write on the blackboard; one sheet will be the ballot you are to take home."

When she retrieved the typewritten page from the desk, the hand in which she held it had become quite steady. Turning to the blackboard she wrote in large, clear letters:

YES NO

☐ ☐ I am in favor of abiding by the decision of the Supreme Court and the Pupil Placement Plan, which is in compliance with the law of the State of Tennessee.

☐ ☐ I am in favor of Mr. Cobb's continued service as principal of Fayette High School.

Harry Nelson let out a loud, poorly fabricated yawn while the teacher's back was turned. When the copying was done and she faced the class again, he cried out, "No, Ma'am! I sure ain't buying that!"

A nervous titter spread through the room but died quickly.

Mrs. Barlow frowned and said tartly, "You can record your opinion on paper, Nelson, like everyone else in this room."

In the buzz of conversation that arose while the blank sheets were being distributed, Robby waited to see if the monitor would pass him by. When she held out the paper to him, he took the two sheets without looking up and said, "Thank you," in a voice that was flat and hardly audible. With a pretense of being unhurried, he began copying from the board. When the task was completed, he checked "yes" in the correct column and signed his name.

The room became full of chatter as the monitors collected the ballots and began to tally them. Robby stared at the sky out of the closed windows and realized that there had been no sound from the pickets for a long time. And as he waited for the result of the vote, sitting upright and rigid, he wondered what would happen if the vote was a great, big NO!

Mrs. Barlow's tap on the desk and her demand for silence interrupted his thoughts. She was smiling faintly when she announced, "Harry Nelson is a minority of one in this class. There were 25 yes votes for each proposition. He cast the only negative vote."

A spontaneous "Hooray!" sparked by Andrew Sinclair was taken up by the class and became a loud, drawn-out shout.

Robby shifted in his seat, as though he had suddenly found more room for himself in the chair. Before the teacher had time to make a comment, the bell clanged. There was a racket of moving chairs and a rush for the door. He hung back and waited for Linda.

Together they walked down the long, quickly emptying corridor, carrying their new books. Robby wanted to talk about the vote, but he had become aware of the sharp click of shoes with metal disks striking the floor close behind them. They were both silent. When they reached the shorter passageway that was entirely empty, the sound of clicking steps close behind increased in number. Robby looked questioningly at Linda, but she was staring straight ahead, and he had no way of knowing if she shared his suspicion. He remembered an old saying: "Don't turn around in time of danger or you may have to run backwards."

Even if he had turned then, it would have been too late. He felt a push between his shoulders, and he stumbled but did not fall. His books spilled noisily on the polished floor, and he saw that Linda's were among them too.

"My, my!" said a voice that tried to sound mincing. "That's no way to take care of books!"

He knew it was Nelson, even before he saw the face. The redhead had two other boys with him, and even in the midst of Robby's turmoil, he was glad when he saw that Joel Saunders was not one of the three. There was a hammering in his head, and a thick fog seemed to be seeping into him. He tried to open his mouth to say something, but changed his mind and instead bent down to help Linda pick up the books. They had retrieved all of them under the silent gaze of the three boys and turned their backs on them again, but the click of the shoes followed.

"Where you niggers going?" Harry Nelson demanded.

"You ain't showing politeness. When a gentleman talks to you, you gotta learn to answer. You hear?" The words were accompanied by a push that was more vicious this time. The books shot out of Robby's arms and scattered wildly as he lost his balance and fell. From his prone position on the floor, he realized that Linda lay beside him, face down.

"We don't want coons stinking up our school. We're gonna cut your gizzards out if you two don't get out," said Nelson.

Robby was on his feet before he could think, holding out his hands to Linda. He heard a second voice command, "You pick up those nice clean books offa that dirty floor."

There was the yellow stain of a smashed egg oozing over a book lying open on its back. Now that he was on his feet, Robby asked himself wildly what he must do. Go for Nelson first? He was as big as the redhead and stronger; he could kill him if he got his hands around his white neck. But Robby stood there and did nothing, as he listened through the hammering in his head to Howie saying, *"Keep out of fights, relax and make like you're a sack of meal."*

A teacher appeared in the hallway, and the attackers fled. Robby pulled out a handkerchief and wiped the slimy blob from the book. He knew he should be feeling proud of himself and of his cause—the white boys were the cowards, not he; yet he was unable to look into Linda's face. He wanted to ask her if she was hurt, but the words would not come. They picked up all the books, and as they walked on, Robby felt her fingers reaching for his.

"You don't have to worry about me," she said softly. "I wasn't hurt. They picked on you because they know you're the leader."

CHAPTER TWELVE

R EVEREND MATTHEW LOGAN was unusually silent through dinner. His wife, Caroline, saw that he toyed with his food and did not even touch the ice-cold chocolate pie which was his favorite dessert.

"You have been getting more worried looking every day," Mrs. Logan said anxiously, "since Abbott brought that stranger to you. Things seem to be getting worse all the time, aren't they, Matthew?"

Logan looked at her with affection, aware of her sympathy, and thought how astonished she would be to learn how much more he was preoccupied with himself than with Collins.

"There must always come a time of reckoning," he replied cryptically, his chin lowered and his thoughts turned inward. When he spoke again, it was as if he were thinking out loud: "I am sure that deep in his heart Cain knew the answer before he asked if he was his brother's keeper. Most of us know when we commit evil. Carrie, I, too, have lived with that sin. I have been pretending to myself that Jameson is something special in this part of the country, but Collins has forced me to admit that it is not an island sealed off from the rest of the world."

"Can't that man be stopped from stirring people up?" his wife asked, unable to follow the drift of what he was saying.

"Unfortunately, my dear," he replied, meeting her perplexed look, "our troubles are not entirely of his making, and therefore the situation cannot be changed so easily. I got a call this morning from the colored minister in Mount Olive. He said that when Collins walked out of jail yesterday, there were several of his friends waiting to greet him; among them was Jay Ford, a Klan leader who lives in Birmingham. And that's quite a way from Jameson. I can just see Collins coming out of the courthouse yesterday afternoon, preening himself, waving and smiling to his followers. I am giving you an exact picture of what happened."

"There's something you must explain to me," Mrs. Logan said, her voice edged with impatience. "Why are the colored people making so much fuss about everything *now*? We're good to them here; we live close together, and we understand them better than white people up North. My grandfather

117

used to tell me that he took care of his slaves as if they were his own children. As long as I can remember, we got along peacefully with them. What has happened to change all that? Why can't it remain the way it was?"

"Your grandfather would never have thought it a human trait to sell one of his own children to a slave master," he said with a wry smile, "but that is exactly what he did."

The swinging pantry door opened and Beulah, the cook and maid-of-all work, plodded in heavily on her flat feet to clear the dishes. Mrs. Logan stared at the elderly woman who had worked and lived under their roof as long as she had been married to Matthew. The minister's wife peered into Beulah's shiny black face with silent intensity, as though seeking the answer there. When the maid left the room, Logan continued, "I, too, have asked myself the same question. The only honest conclusion anyone can come to is that our relations with the Negroes have never been either good or peaceful. Not for them and not for us. It only appeared that way because we had to believe it for our own comfort."

Logan seemed to have come out of himself as he went on with sudden passion in his voice. "We have, in fact, been living under a shaky truce since the Civil War but never in peace. It's a long story, Carrie, why the colored people make such loud demands these days, but if more of us knew the real reasons, Collins wouldn't get to first base in this town." He looked at his wristwatch, remembering that he was due at Cobb's house by eight.

"But, Matthew, do *you* know?" Mrs. Logan persisted,

realizing that he was leaving her question unanswered.

"The Barlows are waiting for me at Bill's," he said, going around to kiss her cheek. "Everybody is in something of a panic at this stage. I must run off now."

Reverend Logan had always felt more comfortable with Daisy and William Cobb than with anyone else in Jameson. Their home was a familiar and enjoyable place to him. For many years Caroline and he made up an inseparable foursome with the Cobbs at bridge, and they went on vacation trips together.

When he rang the Cobbs' bell, he was uncertain of his welcome. He tried to brush away the feeling, but his discomfort remained. He was certain that after tonight's meeting he would not be welcome here again.

Mrs. Cobb opened the door. Her greeting was polite but empty of warmth as she let him into the hall.

"Bill is in the living room with Mary Barlow," she said, averting her eyes from his face. "Her husband couldn't come. I know you people don't need me for your meeting, so you won't mind if I go upstairs."

Effusively, hypocritically, Logan said, "Well, now, I'm not so sure we couldn't use your help, too!" He knew he was being dishonest, for Daisy had never made a secret of her opposition to any compromise that would let the Negro children into Fayette, and she had never completely reconciled herself to her husband's involvement with the committee. Daisy simply met the problem by refusing to accept the idea of any legal necessity to conform and looked upon their work as foolish and wrongheaded.

Logan was ashamed of himself now for his posturing and let her go away without another word. He found Mary Barlow and Cobb listening to the eight o'clock TV report coming in from Knoxville and joined them with a silent nod. At once he became fascinated by Collins' face on the screen as he heard him boast with an arrogance which was already familiar that a thousand White Crusade followers would assemble in Courthouse Square at sundown on Wednesday. Wise parents, Collins predicted significantly, would keep their children out of Fayette tomorrow morning to be out of range of trouble.

Cobb switched off the TV with a motion that revealed his disturbed state of mind.

"Good Lord!" Mrs. Barlow exclaimed, breaking the tense silence. "Parents who hadn't the faintest idea of keeping their children out tomorrow are certainly giving it serious consideration at this minute! That free broadcast helps the White Crusade just as much as if they had paid real money for spreading their propaganda."

"You're quite right," Cobb said quickly. "It's helped him recruit not only in the county but out-of-state people, too. We have also used the TV to get our program across," he added irritably, "but we have yet to learn how much it has worked in our favor."

"Where is Walter tonight?" Logan interjected. "We need his good judgment at a time like this."

The query threw Mary Barlow into confusion. She had

just seen the evidence on TV of how fears could be crassly manipulated among the unwary, but now she would have to reveal how she too had succumbed to the hysteria Collins was whipping up. She began her explanation timidly, with worried eyes.

"When Walter left his office this evening, he saw Collins haranguing a crowd in the Square; they were mostly men from the mill and the coal yard. Instead of their going right home, they stopped to take a look and stayed to listen. Walter thinks there's the kind of excitement brewing downtown that we have when the carnival comes here; but he's afraid it won't remain harmless like that." It embarrassed her to be taking so long to give her reply, and she went on uncomfortably, "Since that anonymous Sunday phone call, we don't like to leave Lester and Jane alone. I didn't want to frighten them by calling in a neighbor . . . Walter told the children he had a headache and didn't want to go out." She tried to smile. "We haven't used a baby-sitter for a long time. . . I know it's silly, and I'm exaggerating."

"I don't think you're exaggerating," Cobb said crossly. "I hope you take what is happening here as seriously as it should be taken." His face had never looked as troubled as it did now, and his voice sounded aggrieved. "We should all be more concerned than we are," he added. "I asked you to come here tonight because I will not take responsibility for what happens at my school unless some strong measures are taken to restore order in town. I've already arranged for a full conference at the mayor's office for tomorrow evening. We three and Walter have been a sort of committee within a committee; I've followed your advice until now, and before we go to that meeting, we've got to figure out how to end this impossible situation."

Logan was not altogether unprepared for Cobb's behavior, which seemed to accuse everyone in Jameson of conspiring against his personal well-being, but he felt his way carefully.

"Walter was quite right to stay with the children, if it makes you feel easier," he said, "though I am inclined to agree that you may be making more of the phone call than it warrants. But Bill is correct in saying that we must put a stop to Collins' agitation before it goes any further."

"Wasn't there some way to keep him in jail," Mrs. Barlow interrupted, "or send him packing as soon as we found out what he was up to? I must admit I'm not very optimistic now about the usefulness of the balloting we began this morning."

"The damage was done before Collins was arrested," Cobb broke in shrilly. "It wouldn't have helped even if we had driven him out of town the morning school opened, because he had already made contact with Ford and the others. From what I see going on, I feel like you; I doubt if we had a majority of the people with us when we opened those doors on Monday."

"Oh, I didn't mean that!" Mrs. Barlow protested with alarm.

Cobb paid no attention to the interruption. "I was willing to go along and give the plan a chance, but I don't know . . .

men do not give up their belief because some cooked-up law demands it of them. Don't forget that in Virginia, right across the border from Washington, where that law was made, all public schools are closed because some people stick to their principles."

Logan saw the appeal in Mary Barlow's eyes as she turned to him for help. He knew that Bill had misunderstood her completely. "I don't think Mary doubts the fact that we have a majority of the people with us," he said. "What she meant was only the timing of the voting. It is quite true," he went on, "that a man's beliefs are all-important to him. They are the moral justification for his acts; we would not be human without them. And I agree with you, Bill, that our problem in Jameson is not to be solved by force alone. But there is something we can use to strengthen our position which until now has been ignored. I mean the force of morality."

Logan spoke rapidly, as though fearful of being stopped. "It has taken me a long time—far too long—to face up to the fact that our position will remain untenable as long as it rests only on the *legality* of our plan. Laws always lag far behind men's needs; usually until the old ways are outlived and become harmful, because most people are so afraid of change. Although it appears that we have been naive not to have expected trouble in Jameson, we are not simpletons. What we did was to blind ourselves so that everything might seem reasonable and sound. For three hundred years our minds have been closed to the truth of the Negro's position in our country; and when people have no alternatives with which to temper their views, they are easily misled and what appears to be righteousness is only great error."

Logan saw Mary Barlow's eager concentration on his words and took courage. He was close enough to Bill to know the rigidness of his friend's views—he would close his mind to what was disturbing for him to hear and use anger and resentment as a shield against any challenge to his moral infallibility. He got up and began to pace the floor, determined to speak whether Cobb listened or not. At least Mary would try to understand what he was saying.

"My own guilt is very great in this crisis," he continued, "because in a minister the sin of self-deception is unforgivable. A thoroughgoing change is taking place all over the world. The meek are truly beginning to inherit the earth. It was bound to come, of course, and we are pathetically unprepared for it. What is happening in Africa and Asia has profoundly influenced the colored people of our country—especially the young. Their lives can never again be the same as that of their parents."

Logan stopped in his pacing. "We must have the courage to begin our campaign all over again!" he cried. "We must state with forthrightness that it is the Christian right of Negro children to sit in the same classroom with white boys and girls. When we have said that, the evil subterfuge of token enrollment will fall of its own weight. Let us declare that the moral right comes first. The legal right is only secondary. Collins knows that we are on thin ice here and takes full advantage of that fact. Our way has been either to say to the

Negro child, 'You are not yet ready for brotherhood,' or like Collins, 'You will never be ready.' Of the two, the so-called middle-of-the-way sin is the greater, because it is self-deluding —because the truth is that we resist violently any attempt of the Negro family to achieve equality of opportunity. Without equality of opportunity, they can never escape from ignorance, poverty, and degradation."

Logan added quietly, "I am most guilty of wrongdoing. I have known all this a very long time, but chose to remain silent. I sought refuge from controversy by perverting my conscience, telling myself that we whites were not ready for change." He strode over to the unshaded window and turned his back upon the room, his hands clasped behind him, as he added, "On Sunday I shall bear witness. . . ."

"You can stop right there!" Cobb's voice was so harsh with anger that Logan swung around to face him. "I'm glad you finally spoke your real mind, Matthew. Now I can tell you what I think. I was suspicious of your intentions in this school business when it got started, but I fooled myself by thinking we wanted the same thing. What you just said makes everything clear. If I thought that letting those eight kids into my school was a way of helping a conspiracy to destroy our way of life, I would resign my job today. I have no intention of telling any colored man that he is my equal. It will take a long time—if ever—for them to reach our development. I went along with the plan, as everyone knows, as a way of holding the line until something better shows up."

Cobb was also standing now, and the two men faced each

other across the length of the room. "The only thing that keeps me on your side so far," he added, "is that I won't be pushed around by a white mob any more than by niggers or Communists. I'm ready to bargain with you. Don't make the mistake of putting wrong ideas into people's heads that can do great damage. . . . I'm giving you the chance to prove that my suspicions were wrong. Your only job, and mine, is to put the White Crusade out of action."

"Wait, Bill!" Mrs. Barlow pleaded. "Let me tell you what Walter says before Reverend Logan answers. He too has begun to think that our way is wrong and can't succeed because it isn't much different from what the White Crusade says. Walter also thinks that there must be some better way!"

Cobb's face became more flushed, but he ignored the interruption. "I advise you, Matthew, not to say anything from your pulpit to stir up more trouble in town. Our first job is to keep law and order from breaking down. You have no right to agitate for your radical views any more than Collins has. If you want me to stick to my part of the bargain, you'll have to leave things alone. Do you understand?"

Logan was only too well aware of the impasse they had reached. He did not want to hurt the man who was his friend, so he said gently, trying to soften the blow, "Bill, the time has come to tell my congregation what I think is the truth. Unhappily, 'truth' is one of the most tortured words in the language of man. The very things we cannot see with our eyes, simply because of our own limited knowledge, is what makes the difference in judging what is true and what is false. Those who hear what I must tell them may reject what I say, but at least I will have begun to do my duty. I can provide them with some possibility of testing their beliefs against fact instead of a mirage. But I don't see why that should prevent us from going to the meeting you planned with the mayor and finding the means to uphold the law."

"I'm sure it isn't hopeless, Bill!" Mary Barlow intervened. "Let's try to do the job for which you brought us here. A break in our ranks will only give aid to our opponents. Between now and Sunday something can be done to at least bring the situation back to where it was before Collins got here."

Logan nodded to the logic of the plea and added eagerly, "Collins can be re-arrested on an order from Knoxville and kept out of town. Even Jay Ford isn't invulnerable. Both of us can do what we believe to be right. Only testing can prove the correctness of our different views."

Cobb's face was unrelenting. "There's no use discussing it any more tonight," he said coldly. "I may be able to do better with the full committee tomorrow. But there is one thing I want to make clear in advance—I am not ready to surrender a way of life my forefathers found good and have cherished over the centuries. I will protect myself against rabble-rousers of any color."

CHAPTER THIRTEEN

C OBB PREFERRED DRIVING to walking, but he set
out on foot Wednesday evening to avoid the tangle of out-of-
town traffic which was clogging the downtown area. He was
acutely aware of the change which had taken place in Jameson overnight. It could be seen and felt even in Crestwood.
Instead of rocking on the front porch after supper, or cutting
their lawns, some of his neighbors were walking in the direction of Courthouse Square; but their gait, unlike his own,
seemed peculiarly without purpose, as though they were not
quite sure of their destination.

When he had gone a short distance from his doorstep,
Cobb nodded gravely to Sam Bennett, walking with his teen-
age son. Bennett smiled uneasily as he explained, "I thought

128

we'd just take a look at what's doing downtown. I hear things were pretty rough at Fayette this morning." He stopped smiling as he added, "I expected it to come to this . . . they say it's getting worse every day. It's a good thing I kept the boy home. . . ."

The principal stopped his neighbor short. "I'm sorry you kept Dick out of school. Nothing would have happened to him if he had attended to his own business. And I must tell you, Bennett, you've got to make up your mind if you're going to let a bunch of hoodlums run the high school or the man appointed to do the job." He strode off, leaving Sam Bennett openmouthed.

Daylight was almost gone when Cobb reached the downtown area. The slow moving cars had their headlights on, and where the highway and county back road fed into Main Street, the traffic poured in at a steady pace. He remembered what Mrs. Barlow said last night about the carnival atmosphere and realized how correct Walter had been. The excitement and expectation in the air felt thick enough to touch. He saw unfamiliar faces gaping from car windows to meet the wandering gaze of the local people. At the intersection where the frozen custard kiosk stood in a blaze of neon lights, a long queue was buying cold refreshments in the sultry night; everyone seemed to be waiting for something to happen.

When he reached the periphery of Courthouse Square, the crowd was larger than at a Fourth of July fireworks display. He strained to catch a glimpse of Collins or Ford as he cut across the diagonal path leading to the mayor's office in the red brick building. Curiosity suddenly impelled him to change his course when he saw an unusual concentration of people around the Soldiers and Sailors Monument, and he began to edge his way toward it.

The memorial to the dead was a long, polished block of marble standing four feet high with a flat surface on top. Linked to it at one end loomed a larger-than-life stone figure of a World War II soldier, standing at his perpetual ease. The legend on the face of the monument read:

IN MEMORY OF OUR NOBLE DEAD WHO GAVE
THEIR LIVES THAT FREEDOM MIGHT LIVE

Cobb recalled that there were eleven names of local boys chiseled into that marble. With increased agitation, he remembered the controversy over the list. Three of those names belonged to Negro dead. It came back to him now with sudden meaning: Matthew Logan was responsible for their inclusion; and it was Logan who invited the Negro choir to sing at his church at about the same period.

Cobb was jolted as he realized how skillfully the minister had disguised his aim of subverting Jameson's cherished values and traditions.

A burly man in a plaid shirt blocked his path and interrupted Cobb's train of thought. The man was shouting, "Join the White Crusade!" Holding high a small white pasteboard sign, he bellowed, "Sign here with a red-blooded organization of white folks!"

A placard on a pole stuck in the grass near him read:

The principal winced at the misspelled word. He saw that the top of the monument was being used as a recruiting desk, and a young matron bent over it to sign a membership card. As he stared at her, the rancor which Cobb had for Matthew Logan now included Ford and Collins, who were somewhere in this crowd pulling the strings the way Matthew did—all of them bringing disaster upon the town. But he blamed the minister most; it was he who had given these outsiders the opportunity to stir up the weak-minded, white and black, for his own inscrutable aims. Cobb blamed Logan for his loss of peace of mind; for the attempt to destroy the dignity of his school office; and most of all, for the loss of a once-valued friendship.

The principal was the last of the committee members to arrive in the mayor's high-ceilinged conference room on the second floor. Here he found Whitney and Police Commissioner Roland at an open window watching the crowd below. Mayor Whitney, a man with pink skin and snow-white hair, pounced upon Cobb at once.

"What do you think of that turnout, Bill?" he asked rhetorically. "I wouldn't have believed it possible to whip up an attendance this size in such a short time."

"It blew up over night," interjected Commissioner Roland. "Most of them are from other parts." He sounded apologetic, as though the guilt for the large crowd was his.

Before Cobb had an opportunity to say anything, the

mayor led the way to the long mahogany table in the middle of the room. Overhead an old-fashioned ceiling fan spun noisily. Mrs. Barlow was already seated between her husband and Reverend Logan. Hector Lawrence, Jameson's leading real estate and insurance broker, who was president of the school board, sat opposite Whitney's presiding chair. William Cobb took the unoccupied seat near John Sinclair of the *Courier;* he found himself directly opposite Logan.

Whitney had to raise his voice to be heard above the whir of the fans. He spoke informally from his seat.

"To put it bluntly, friends," he began gloomily, "it looks as though we have been caught flatfooted. Even if Bill Cobb had not asked for this meeting, I was ready to bring you all here. It's quite clear that we must examine everything with a fresh eye." He turned to the principal of Fayette High. "I think we ought to hear from you first, Bill. I know you want to get a few things off your chest."

Cobb would have preferred to have others speak first so they could smoke out Logan's views and thereby make his own task of denouncing the minister more telling. But he did not hesitate to launch his offensive.

"I don't pretend to know just where we miscalculated," he began. "There may be others, like Reverend Logan, for example, who profess to know the answer. I'm sure he will enlighten you soon enough. In my opinion, the Placement Plan is still our only solution at this time. We will not let a mob stand in the way of its success. But it has become obvious that our own law enforcement machinery cannot cope with the situation. I want to keep Fayette open, but unless there is extra police protection tomorrow morning, I refuse to take responsibility for opening its doors. It was a mistake in the first place to pick up Collins under an ordinance that couldn't stick. We need a federal order for his arrest. . . ." Cobb saw Hector Lawrence raise a right index finger, and although he had not completed his speech, he yielded at once to the president of the school board.

Lawrence, a well-groomed, middle-aged man, thanked Cobb with a gesture and began to speak slowly. "I would seriously advise against being hasty about involving the federal government in Collins' arrest. Once you give these people an opportunity to step in, we begin to lose whatever authority we have over the management of our own affairs. To my knowledge, he has not yet done anything but exercise his right of free speech; and as far as Jay Ford from Alabama is concerned, no one knows of his having committed an illegal act here."

"How can you possibly say that?" Mrs. Barlow broke in with dismay. "Collins and Ford are inciting people to break the law. Surely the decent citizens need some protection against them—especially Collins. The mob in front of Fayette this morning was terrifying! The colored students made their way through it with great bravery, but dozens of our children were kept home by their parents. I'm afraid to think of what will happen tomorrow as a result of what's going on in the Square at this very moment."

Walter Barlow quickly backed up his wife. "Hector, you

will be interested to know," he said with quiet intensity, "that we asked a neighbor to sit with our kids so that we could both come here tonight. I for one see a dangerous situation developing. It has gotten beyond the wait-and-see stage. I'm interested in more than just Collins' arrest. If my wife is to be in her class tomorrow, I insist that we get extra police protection, and I don't care if it comes from the federal government or the North Pole. After that, it's up to the lawyers to figure out a way of handling the mob leaders. I'm for going after all of them fast!"

"There is a second priority," Cobb put in. "Somebody is to blame for egging on the colored people and causing all this racial strife. When we find out just who is behind it, things will become a lot easier to settle. There are certain radical ideas being pushed in town that need airing right at this table. The idea, for instance, that the colored man has the God-given right to move into my social club if he wants to. Or that every white man in Jameson grinds the Negro down like a slave. Why, even in the days of my great-grandfather, who had hundreds of them, a Southern gentleman treated all blacks with consideration. I understand that Reverend Matthew Logan would like to turn over control of Jameson to the colored folks. I'm sure he can explain it all to you."

Cobb's challenge produced the shock in his listeners which he had intended to achieve, and all eyes turned expectantly toward the minister.

"I am thankful for this opportunity to speak," Logan said, his heart heavy with the knowledge of Cobb's bitterness toward him. "Our most serious problem is that until now we have been most unwilling to air certain ideas. One of them has to do with slaveholding.

"Unfortunately, even the best slave owners looked upon the Negro not as a human being but as a tool of labor, and we have been doing our utmost to perpetuate that image ever since. Bill's great-grandfather gave his full support to a law which said it was a crime for a slave to be taught to read and write. Bill's ancestor was a cultivated, civilized, and God-fearing man who could not permit himself to believe that a slave was a human being like himself; otherwise how could he work black men, women, and children profitably—on the same level with horses and oxen? It would be too much to expect such a man to equate his own humanity with that of his chattel and at the same time condone slavery."

"Aren't we getting far afield from the matter that brought us here?" Lawrence interrupted equably. No one else seconded the protest, and Logan continued quietly.

"If we are to understand where today's racial strife began, we must take a long look backward. The black man is given no choice but to do menial labor, and then we insist that he is unfit for anything better. We place every obstacle in the way of the Negro child's normal development, and then we say he is not the equal of the white student. This evil is self-perpetuating. . . ."

Cobb shook his head violently. "You can never prove that," he cried. "The evidence of our eyes tells us differently. If we gave them all the opportunities in the world, they would still be lazy, shiftless, and without ambition. They have yet to prove—with rare exceptions—they can benefit by any more education than they now get."

"I am strongly convinced," Logan answered, "that the colored people no longer think that they must prove anything to the white man. They ask *us* to prove that we can fulfill the promise of emancipation. If we fail in this, they will some day take their rights by force."

Cobb broke in jubilantly. "Well, Matthew, now we know where you stand! What you advocate is bloody insurrection. It's too bad you didn't tell us this a long time ago. I don't know what the others here feel, but if you carry out the threat you made to me privately to expound these views in your pulpit, I will oppose you all the way and see that your ideas don't take root in this town! There is only one thing that keeps me at the same table with you at this moment; that is the necessity of putting down the rule of the mob. There must be a showdown on that. But if you persist in subverting our citizens, we can handle that also."

In the stunned silence that followed this exchange, Logan realized that at last he had chosen to take a step toward his own freedom. He sighed deeply. Cobb had misunderstood him completely, but he felt a sudden release and a great sense of freedom. It surprised him now how unreal was the fear he once had of losing his pulpit or his position of honor and authority. The important thing was that he had entered on the only path which could lead him to true salvation.

136

"Opening up that kind of talk," said the mayor, the first to recover his speech, "doesn't help us much at this moment. Let's face it, we're on the spot, but getting into discussions over what happened three hundred years ago isn't much good now. The only hopeful factor I see in what has been said is that we pretty well agree on the need to get the White Crusade and Collins out of the picture and return to the *status quo ante*. As long as Fayette stays open—and it has got to stay that way—the kids who go to school have the right to our protection. I think we can provide it, if we are able to recruit a minimum of twenty-five deputized officers to be on hand tomorrow morning."

Commissioner Roland, who had been doodling nervously on a scratch pad, put his pen down with a bang.

"I'm also for action and less talk at a time like this. Let's take care of the mob first. The place to get our deputies is at the hydroelectric plant at Telford. I wouldn't try to swear in anyone else but federal workers."

"That's out of the question!" cried Hector Lawrence, no longer leisurely in speech. "I'm opposed to unnecessarily involving a federal agency in this. I see no necessity for it. The wisest step would be to close Fayette until things are quiet again. We can get back to normal faster that way."

Barely holding his temper in check, John Sinclair entered the dispute.

"All you will accomplish by closing the high school is to inform Collins that *he* is in control here. I'm even in favor of asking Washington for armed troops in a show of force, if deputies aren't enough. If anyone still thinks we can reverse the steps already taken, he is quite mistaken. To try that, is only to encourage anarchy and chaos."

William Cobb had kept his eyes lowered upon the shiny table as he listened to the discussion he had started. He was not afraid of Sinclair, whose public and private position on race-mixing had never gone a hair's breadth beyond a middle-of-the-road program. Unlike Logan, he said openly that colored people were too childlike and inexperienced for the responsibility of full citizenship. Sinclair could be trusted. Cobb saw clearly that if it came to a showdown in the committee, those who were for law and order would have to side, not with Hector Lawrence, but with the majority, of which Logan was still a member.

The discussion continued to go against the school board president so decisively that the need for a vote on recruiting the deputies was not even considered. Sinclair volunteered to drive to Telford immediately with Commissioner Roland. "If we bring them back here by early morning," the editor urged, "we could have that information on television and radio by the time Jameson drinks its breakfast coffee. That bit of news could put some kind of brake on certain hotheads right away and give us a chance during the day to work on Collins and Ford."

Cobb brought the talk back to Logan by reminding them of the minister's threat to preach his radical views from his pulpit on Sunday. "We must have his promise not to upset the apple cart," Cobb said.

Whitney added his own cautiously worded protest. "We have more pressing things to do," he asserted, "than to indulge in religious debate at this moment; although I don't deny that it may have its usefulness at a later date, when we have things in hand again. But it would be wrong to say anything in church now that might stir up more people." The mayor considered the subject closed and announced that he would ask Knoxville to provide a federal warrant for the re-arrest of Collins. The big clock on the wall began to chime nine o'clock, as he hastily put his official stamp of approval to the recruitment of deputies at Telford.

"The meeting is closed," he declared. "Let's go down there and see what's happening. That crowd sounds as if it's gotten much bigger."

The commissioner and Sinclair left at once to make the thirty-mile trip to Telford, knowing that the task of getting together a contingent of deputized men overnight and bringing them back to Jameson by morning was not going to be easy.

Down in the Square, in tow of his friend Harry, Joel Saunders stood in a privileged spot at the foot of the speakers' platform, gazing up at Collins, who stood alone under an improvised spotlight. Squeezed around him was the entire Drake family, the Abbotts, and Prowse and his wife. Except for the occasional distant honk of a horn, the speaker's amplified voice filled the air with its incisive words. An American flag hung limply on its pole in the still, warm night.

Collins' arms were spread wide as he warned, "Wake up to your danger! There are almost twenty million colored in this country. If you don't want to be drowned by the black tide, something's got to be done about it right here in Jameson. And quick, too!"

Joel looked sideways at Harry Nelson, then hopefully at Drake, then at Prowse and Jason Abbott, seeking a clue in their faces to the significance of those words. But the rapt attention with which they were listening told him nothing. He saw Mayor Whitney, with Mr. Cobb and Mrs. Barlow, standing on the Courthouse steps listening to Collins. Their presence made him conscious of a line drawn between two camps —those who were on the side of the White Crusade and those against it. But he had no feeling of being on either side.

Collins pounded a fist into the palm of his hand as he cried, "The time has come to show that the people are greater than the fossils of the Supreme Court. If the old men who run this town have no guts—if they don't know how to protect the white woman, her home, and her children—it's up to us to show them how."

The crowd whistled and cheered its approval. Before the applause subsided, a voice yelled, "A stick of dynamite in the right place might show them."

Collins' arms shot forward with his palms downward, in a calming gesture. "No, my friends, that's not the way. We're going to *persuade* the politicians that they are wrong. We're going to do it peacefully. I know you aren't afraid to light a fire under them; but we don't need that yet. We can *con-*

vince the bureaucrats that even if the nigger jimmies his way into our schools he can't force himself into our hearts. Nobody living has the right to tell you whom to love."

Harry Nelson dug an elbow into Joel's ribs. "How about that?"

Joel nodded automatically and stretched forward toward the speaker on the platform to listen more closely.

"We're not going to bend the knee to traitors in our midst!" Collins screamed.

The crowd was with him, enjoying his fervid pronouncements which blended forcefully with his fancy gymnastics. The skillfulness with which he kneaded words together with the movement of his body helped to obscure the poverty of his ideas. Ben's theme was simple, but the variations with which he could express it seemed infinite and ever fresh to his listeners. He was proving himself an orator. When he had elaborated and embellished his text for half an hour, Collins gave Jay Ford the platform.

Those who recognized the Alabama Klan leader welcomed him with Rebel yells. Ford's voice was like a foghorn, and his neck swelled as he threw himself into his task.

"Folks," he bellowed, "our friend Ben hit the nail on the head. We're not going to be pushed around by this red National Nigger Ass-ociation." He stopped and waited confidently for the crowd to enjoy his humor. "We just ain't going to let nobody come here to stir the nigger up; we're in this together. Where I live we don't have no trouble at all. Our colored folks are peaceable and like to be by themselves. You

141

gotta watch out for Communists and outsiders sneaking in to agitate, and you gotta watch out extra special for white nigger-lovers. They're the worst kind."

Ford's delivery matched the heaviness of his massive body. He could not hold the audience after Collins' long speech, and a part of the crowd began to break off at the edges, drifting off in search of something to provide a climax to the evening.

Harry tugged at Joel. "C'mon," he said, bending his head in the direction of the highway. "There's a bunch over there; let's go see."

Tom Drake, whose attention had also begun to wander, overheard him and yanked at Prowse. "Let's go with them." Only Abbott stayed behind with the womenfolk. They made their way slowly toward the spot where diversion seemed to be in the making. When they reached the northbound lane, they found a gang of men surrounding a passenger car with tightly shut windows. Even in the dark, Joel could see the scared faces of a Negro man and woman in the front seat and a small boy and girl in the back. The besiegers had already ripped off much of the trimming from the shiny Pontiac. They had removed the gasoline cap, windshield wipers, and hub caps. They were working to pull off the Pennsylvania license plate.

The new arrivals tried to pitch in. Joel made an effort to get his hands on the car, but there were too many prior claimants in his way, so he gave it up as not worth the effort. When the license came off, the gang began to rock the car and its occupants like a cradle.

Joel looked with curiosity at the frenzied, whooping exertions of the men but kept his hands deep in his pockets. Again he caught a glimpse of the dazed, wide-eyed looks on the faces of the family in the car and was suddenly filled with distaste for the sport, but he remained glued to the spot.

"Open those windows," he heard Drake shout, pounding on the glass. "We want to talk to you."

The man in the car kept his hands on the wheel and sat like a carved image. The rocking was already becoming monotonous to the men when a town constable arrived.

"That's enough, boys," he said, keeping up the fiction that it was all in fun. "Let them go. I don't know how they got through our lines." He motioned to the driver of the car, who had not shut off the motor during the ordeal. He gunned it now, and the car shot clear of the mob.

Joel felt a sudden relief when he saw the Pontiac leap into freedom; it seemed like the only possible outcome of the game. He was beginning to have the unpleasant feeling that too many strangers were in town tonight, taking Jameson over and keeping it out of the hands of the home team. And suddenly it struck him that all the noise and excitement they were blowing up made the play against Robby Jones and his seven colored friends so unequal that there just was no game at all. Anyway, he didn't believe they could change the law.

Although the car and its occupants were out of reach, the gang still showed no sign of breaking up, but stood around aimlessly. The opportunity for action came when someone shouted, "Dig that coon at the bus station. Let's get him!"

The young Negro standing alone on the sidewalk was fair game; he was an outsider, or he would not be downtown tonight.

"Let's get him!" yelled Prowse. "We don't want no agitators here."

The men howled joyfully as they set off in pursuit. Harry Nelson was well in the lead, with Tom Drake and Prowse, despite their age, not far behind. Joel ran, too, keeping his eyes fixed on the fleeing Negro. He did not know why he was running, until he saw the dozen hands fasten on the panting man. Only then did he realize that he had to see how it ended. Harry preempted the right of grabbing the small zipper bag the youth carried and scattering its contents on the ground. The others ripped off the young man's outer clothing and left him his underwear and shoes. When they loosened their hold, Tom Drake gave the Negro a vicious kick.

"We'll put a rope around your neck," he said, "if you ever come back here."

It was nearing ten o'clock when they all trooped back to the Square. The crowd had dwindled to less than fifty people, but the speechmaking was continuing in the person of a scrawny little man in a wrinkled frock coat and stiff collar. Joel saw that Arlene, Jenny, their mother, Mrs. Prowse, and the Abbotts were still there; but Mrs. Barlow and her friends were gone.

The little man spoke in a thin high voice which seemed to stretch near breaking point as he screamed, "You will find no equality after death. The Christian goes up into heaven, and everyone else goes down into burning hell. God never did create his creatures equal, or he wouldn't have made some men black. All the foolishness about equality makes me sick! In this town we have a minister preaching equality. That man has forgotten about the salvation of the immortal soul and is up to his neck in politics, joining Communistic organizations that divide our churches and our people. He is the devil in our midst."

The little man stopped for breath, and when he spoke again, his voice was whining. "Everybody knows that niggers ain't no more than grown-up children. Folks, you show me where the Bible says that the black man and the white man are equal, and I'll eat my Sunday-go-to-meeting hat. I want you to understand that I feel a deep affection for some colored people I know. You love your child, but your child ain't your equal."

The speaker's last words were to urge his remaining listeners to show up in front of Fayette High in the morning to defeat the devil. Collins took the spotlight again to wind up the meeting.

"We expect all of you to turn out," he said. "Let's show them that this is still the land of the free and the home of the brave."

The flagpole was taken down by his lieutenants, and the speakers' platform dismantled and carried off. Jason Abbott pumped Ben Collins' hand, congratulated him on the success of the rally, and proudly drove him back to the shelter of his home.

Joel walked home alone. It had been a much busier evening than he had expected. He remembered his promise to Harry to be at a meeting with Collins tomorrow after school. His lips had said "Yes" to Nelson, but his mind had said "Maybe."

CHAPTER FOURTEEN

W<small>HEN BEN COLLINS</small> wound up his rally in
Courthouse Square, the nightly conference of the eight Negro
students with Reverend Wilkins and Howard Carter was also
over. The young people and their Carver friends were sprawled
on the thin grass in front of the A.M.E. Zion Church. They
had been able to hear echoes of that rally on their hilltop, and
though it reached them only faintly, what it said to some was
louder than thunder.

But Robby was not among those whom the rally frightened. He lay on the ground with his hands behind his head,
staring into the night sky, and he was filled with a strange
kind of joy. For the first time since Monday morning, he was
moving completely under his own steam. There was nothing

else mixed in with his need—not the desire to please Howie, or Reverend Wilkins, or to prove anything to anyone. As he gazed at the mysterious profusion of stars overhead, his elation increased. For paradoxically, while he was on his own, he felt at this very moment linked to Negroes everywhere who were struggling with him. He was bound to millions of black people, all moving together toward their common goal. He was a part of them, and their strength filled him with a tingling, shivery, new kind of joy.

He understood Rosa Parks better now; how one day she just would not let them herd her to the back of the bus, after she had paid the same fare as white people. The newspapers said she was a frail little woman, but it was she who had set in motion a movement that now reached into his own life. He was a part of her victory, and Robby felt a lump rising in his throat as he thought of the miracle Mrs. Parks had wrought.

The rally in the Square was at this moment almost a matter of indifference to him. The principal of Fayette had been informed about the organized gang in the school, and he promised Reverend Wilkins to set up a student monitoring system. That gang did not worry Robby tonight. There seemed to be nothing the white people could do to alter the course on which he had started. But this strange mood of self-satisfaction was roughly jarred when Joyce Baker shook him.

"You know my dad told me I couldn't come tonight," she said loudly. "But Mom is still on my side. Daddy says he can make me go up North to school because I'm a minor; but

I'm sticking right here with you!" She tossed her black, silky hair as she looked around for approval.

"You got it wrong, girl," Robby said peevishly, as he was brought back to earth. "What you should say, is 'up South'!" he added.

"You'd be the first to go to New York if you had the chance," she retorted.

"I would not!" He sat up to face her. "Since when did old Jim Crow move out of Harlem, anyway? Even in New York, any white boozer can live in a building where they won't let a colored preacher in at the front door."

"Just the same," drawled Amos, "my uncle Daniel is a waiter in a big joint in Chicago, and he says the only way they can get him to go back to Mississippi is in a coffin."

"That's not because he's got it so good there," Linda joined in. "He thinks it's a lot worse back home, that's why!"

Jerry Moore, lying on his stomach, his thin face cupped between his hands, sat up and entered the argument with sudden ferocity.

"I bet colored people in Harlem would show more guts than we do if they were in our shoes right now. Howie talks big about times being so different, but he didn't say anything tonight about *our* doing something before they dive-bomb us. If it was okay for one of those white goons to flash a blade at me yesterday, right in their school, then I'm taking my penknife along for company tomorrow. Howie and Reverend Wilkins don't have to know about it." He stretched out again, this time flat on his back. He raised one knee, and the long leg that he crossed over it swung up and down as he lapsed into silence.

There was an incredulous gasp from most of his listeners.

"You gone crazy or something?" Robby asked in amazement. "What do you want to do—shoot up the place? I thought you understood what nonviolent fighting means! We're supposed to fight them by *not* hitting back. Isn't that what we were taught? We just got to take punishment until they see we mean business about getting our rights. We got to show how those white kids act like gorillas, not us! Anyway, you *know* it isn't like in the old days when the Klan could get away with the kind of things they used to do."

"Zat so? You tell me why they can't," Jerry said, "and maybe I can catch."

"We got world commitments. . . ."

"Yass boss—what is them things? I'se listening, boss."

"Brother, them is egg-zakly de ting we-all duz seek." Robby dropped the foolish-sounding dialect and added fiercely, "It's got to do with being free! If we don't prove we got democracy in the U.S.A., we get the heave-ho in lots of countries. Everybody knows that."

"I don't know it. And I'm kinda bugged by that there *we*. White folks don't want no part of that 'we.' It's us gotta do all the work; and boy, I don't even know where all the colored folks are at while I'm supposed to be taking punishment for the white man's sins so's he can repent and go to heaven."

"Have it your way," Robby said quietly. "The U.S.A.

belongs to the white people, but it's going to be our funeral too, if they can't prove they got freedom in this here country. They won't be able to sell that free-world stuff to anybody else."

"You ain't sold it to me, either," Jerry replied.

"What about Dr. King?" Linda broke in eagerly. "Let's talk about him. He's done a whole lot through nonviolence. I believe in what he says."

A loose-jointed, seventeen-year-old Carver boy laughed uproariously. "Who dat?" he sputtered. "I'll be too old to get down to that fountain in the Square by the time paleface lets me drink out of it, if I wait on Reverend King. Just because he says something doesn't prove it's so. We haven't tried the other way yet." He doubled his fists in an imitation of delivering a stiff uppercut and punched the air forcefully.

"Do we just wait for something to happen like it did in Columbia?" Jerry put in.

"Man, you really are nuts!" Robby stared at him open-mouthed. "Why bring that up? This isn't Columbia. What's eating you, Jerry? If you take a penknife into Fayette, even if it's for show, we'll all get kicked out. Nobody's going to come up here to try what they did in that place. Those guys down in the Square know we'd fight back with more than just rocks and bottles if they tried what they used to do in the old days. We've got to find a way to live with white people."

"Not me. I can't wait that long," said Jerry.

"What does that mean? You taking your penknife?"

While everyone silently waited for the answer, Jerry stared at the silver-speckled sky and watched a thin cloud as it moved like a billowed sail straight toward the moon. He was waiting for the cloud to touch the moon before he would give them the answer.

But the spell broke when Mr. Tilson came out of the church to take his daughter home with him. Linda got up from the ground.

"What are you going to do, Jerry?" she asked cryptically, to keep her father out of their secret. She could not leave before hearing what Jerry had to say.

Jerry Moore jumped to his feet and doubled over in a paroxysm of laughter. "Jeez! You all must think I'm Dracula," he roared. "I'm going to do what everybody else does. What do you expect?" He bent down and took a stiff playful poke at Robby, rolling him over in the grass.

Lying just as Jerry had rolled him over, his face pressed to the cool earth, Robby thought that there was nothing more to be said about Columbia. It was only a bad dream, which could not happen again anywhere in the U.S.A. Only the grown-ups in Mount Olive remembered, because the killings took place so near them. Jerry and all the rest of the high school boys and girls were in diapers in those days. It was a different world then and nobody could say otherwise.

CHAPTER FIFTEEN

THURSDAY WAS JUST DAWNING when Mr. Cobb received the news by telephone that twenty-five deputies were on their way to Jameson. He made no effort to return to sleep, but dressed slowly and ate his usual breakfast, which he prepared to prove to himself that nothing could for long disrupt the established tidiness of his life. He felt a surge of optimism about the future as he breakfasted alone in the bright, clean kitchen; he was confident that events would now move according to his own will. The first step was to demonstrate that constituted authority could impose order on the rabble. It was a cheering prospect after days of wearing anger and frustration.

But as his car sped through the awakening streets of

153

Crestwood, gloom began to envelop him again. The signs of strain returned to his face. His lips were pursed and his gray eyes filled with exasperation as he thought of those who were conspiring against his peace and serenity. Indignation rose within him, and his ire spread out to include Matthew Logan, Mary Barlow, Collins, and all the Communist wire-pullers and their unwitting dupes in Washington.

It was seven o'clock when the principal's car reached Fayette High. Ben Collins' dark figure was already at the head of a crowd massed in the roadway. The radio and TV had proved to be effective recruiters, and more than half of the promised thousand demonstrators were actually on hand. The Telford men were in civilian clothes; they wore distinguishing white helmets and white armbands and carried billies. Spaced out in a straight line in front of the building, they held positions just below the sidewalk curb to a length of two hundred feet. Behind them in a second line of defense were the six local police. He noted the gleaming red fire engine, with its hose linked to a fire hydrant. The sight of the mob depressed him further, and he set his lips tightly as he drove through a barrage of loud jeers.

Cobb greeted the police commissioner glumly as he got out of his car. Roland's eyes were bloodshot from lack of sleep, and there was a stubble of beard on his face. He introduced Cobb to the Telford captain of the deputies, an ex-marine. The photographers edged in, and the reporters, with press cards in their hats, besieged the principal for a statement. Cobb rushed them off with a curt pronouncement. "I will do everything within my authority to abide by the law. That was my position before Fayette High School opened this term, and that is my position now."

By eight o'clock, when the students began to trickle in, the crowd in front of the school had doubled; half of them were only onlookers, separating themselves automatically by an empty swath of no-man's-land between spectator and participant. The mob in the foreground kept up a steady flow of invectives, while the watchers stared silently.

It was eight-thirty when the Negro students, headed by Robby Jones, arrived at the Fayette sidewalk. The column was shorter than on Monday. A boy and girl were missing. The newsmen and photographers made a dash for the three paired students, and a flashbulb went off in front of Robby's eyes. Questions were shot at him from every side:

"How come there's only six of you kids today?"

"Why did the other two drop out?"

"How they treating you in there, sonny?"

"Tell us why you want to go to Fayette High?"

Robby looked straight ahead, as though he could neither hear nor see them. The white men tried to get answers from others in the column, but were met with the same frozen faces. Robby saw the deputies, conspicuous in their helmets, standing before the yelling mob, but they were of no interest; it was as if they had nothing to do with him. He saw a camera kicked out of the hands of a photographer and heard the cry of approval rising from the blur of white faces. He felt, rather than saw, the newsmen at his heels. As he reached the school entrance, Robby stood aside to let his five companions go forward. He was the last to enter the building and could hear the shouting: "Let's go in there and get 'em out!"

When the doors closed on the Negro students, the cry spread through the crowd with increasing clamor. Commissioner Roland, standing guard at the school entrance, knew it would take only one person making a move in the direction of the building, to galvanize the mob into acting out that cry. He took a step forward and lifted a megaphone to his lips.

"In the name of the law," he declared, "I order you to disperse at once. Go home. Go to your jobs. Don't forget this is a workday, folks." The crowd did not move, and he repeated the appeal a second time.

On the far side of no-man's-land, the spectators began to melt away. But the mob in the foreground did not give. Instead, Ben Collins, flanked by his lieutenants Ford, Prowse, Drake, and Abbott, made a concerted move toward the school.

"We want to send a delegation in to talk to Cobb," Collins shouted. The movement and the words drew the demonstrators at his back along with him in a sudden surge forward. But their timing was late.

Roland had already raised his arm to signal, and the fire hose roared a stream of water which arched and exploded into Collins' ranks, splitting it apart, sending men, women, and young people fleeing from its wide-ranging aim. Within minutes the police commissioner and his men were in control of the street and the Square behind it.

When the students left the windows from which they had witnessed the dispersal of the mob and were in their own seats, Mrs. Barlow realized with alarm that attendance in her homeroom was cut in half.

The bell rang as she became aware of how bewildered her students looked. Automatically, she began the roll call. It seemed to the teacher that only Robby Jones and Linda Tilson gave no sign of what they had just seen. She stared openly at them, marveling at the control which kept their faces empty of all feeling. And while she took the attendance, Mrs. Barlow looked to the future, beyond this day and this week, to a time when all the students would be back and guards were no longer necessary; and she asked herself how much nearer to the warmth of normal human relations with the other students these two would be by then. Even six months later, would the white children have reached more than a cold toleration of the Negroes? Robby and Linda would still be excluded from dances, clubs, and the outings which young people enjoyed together.

This morning the prospect for a solution seemed even more hopeless, because she felt that there was little sentiment outside the school which could help to lead all of them toward something better.

Mrs. Barlow drew herself up stiffly to take up the voting project of the day before. The ballots which had been brought back signed by the parents were collected, and the results, as she had expected, tallied with the confidence vote of the students who were present.

"Yesterday a majority of the student body endorsed Mr. Cobb," she announced. "Yet half of our class is missing today, and the same is probably true of the rest of the school. But we know why. Parents received anonymous phone calls last night—and some misguided friendly ones too—advising them to keep their children out because of a threat of violence. In spite of the absentees, we must consider this vote seriously. Attendance was normal for the first three days of school, and that can only mean one thing: the voting we did yesterday was the true picture of what Fayette students and their parents want."

"Gosh! Mrs. Barlow," Joel Saunders exploded, "guys who make phone calls to scare parents like that are punks. I don't see how a few colored students in Fayette can hurt us. Those people are murdering our football team. We can't start practice until all our men come back!" Joel suddenly grinned sheepishly. "I don't really mean it that way. It isn't the football team that's the most important thing."

The gale of laughter which met the boy's final outburst seemed to blow a great hole in the tense atmosphere. Mrs. Barlow smiled faintly.

"Saunders, you don't need to apologize," she said. "I know you understand that there is more at stake today than football. Your presence here proves your good sense, something which many people are not showing today."

Robby Jones smiled too, inwardly, at a wry pun he was thinking of; perhaps Joel just learned that he could get more kicks out of football than from insulting him. Three days ago he was running with the pack, but for the last two days, Joel kept out of his way when they were in homeroom.

"It seems to me," Mrs. Barlow continued, "we need a little discussion of the idea that a few colored students in Fayette can't hurt us. The truth of the matter is, both white and colored sudents can profit from getting to know each other better."

Robby remembered that his mother had called Mrs. Barlow a good woman. The teacher was really trying, he thought cynically, but he could do fine without getting to know the redhead and all the other white kids any better. Nelson was nowhere to be seen this morning, and he wondered what he and his pals were cooking up. Those goons were to blame for Jerry Moore's unexpected failure to show up for school today. He took a powder rather than face their hate again. That was the answer Jerry wouldn't tell them last night in the argument over the penknife. Joyce Baker was the other victim of the gang. She was probably up North by now, just the way her father wanted it all along. But no one knew why Mrs. Simon Baker gave up the fight without any warning.

The bell began its strident clanging while Mrs. Barlow was talking. She stopped in the middle of a sentence, as her voice was drowned out by the scrape of chairs, the shuffle of feet, and the loud chatter of the boys and girls pushing out of the room.

Robby and Linda held back so they could leave together. When they had to separate in the corridor, he hated to see her go off alone. There were supposed to be monitors around to

159

keep an eye on things, but Robby wasn't sure who they were. The only consolation he had was that Nelson wasn't in the building this morning.

Robby's destination led him into a half-empty corridor through which he walked with measured step, neither slow nor fast, so that anyone watching him would not regard his pace as unusual. He was thinking of Linda's progress to her classroom and almost jostled a white girl who was wearing a flouncy short skirt and dirty canvas shoes. She quickened her step, but when he saw that they were both taking the same direction toward a stairway, he slowed down to keep well behind. The girl turned a corner, and he was relieved that she was out of his path.

Moments later, when he, too, reached the landing at the top of the stairs, the girl was there, her body pressed against the wall.

"Okay," he heard her say in a low voice.

There were four boys waiting on the step below, and he saw that it was too late to save himself. They were all masked with handkerchiefs, only eyes showing, and Robby knew at once that the tallest was Harry Nelson.

"You come with us," the redhead said quietly. "We got something to tell you."

Robby thought it was like a dream he used to have—he was unable to move a muscle of his body, and yet his whole being struggled agonizingly to get away. They came at him in one bound and covered his mouth with their hands, even though he was too paralyzed to utter a sound. They lifted his rigid body from the floor and carried him to a lower landing on the stairway.

By midafternoon, a stranger coming into town, knowing nothing of the early morning riot, would have found Main Street looking no different than it did on any other Thursday. The sky was a clear, brilliant blue, and the old men sat idly on park benches under the shade trees in Courthouse Square. Housewives went in and out of stores; and as usual during a workday, traffic on the highway was thin. Only the people of Jameson felt the deceptiveness of the serene-looking afternoon, which was just an interlude of waiting for night to fall.

Jason Abbott neglected his garage for more pressing affairs and was at home conferring with Collins and the rest of the general staff. Ben seemed greatly exhilarated and moved restlessly about the room while he talked. He was analyzing the morning operation, convincing his rapt listeners that the demonstration had brilliantly served its purpose.

"We've proven that there is a strong and kicking opposition here," he cried. "That was only an exercise for the next action! The news of the hosing they gave our people will spread all over the county, and by evening we're going to have hundreds of new recruits in the Square. You can take my word for it."

While they talked and planned for the evening action, Mrs. Abbott put through telephone calls. Thursday was Susie Carter's half-day off; the baby was on her hands, and there was supper to prepare for the guests, but she managed everything willingly and efficiently, eagerly snatching at scraps of the conference. There were out-of-town people to be seen and some of the men left, but Jason, Collins, and Ford stayed indoors for the rest of the afternoon.

By nightfall Collins' judgment was proven correct. His followers had worked feverishly making contacts in the county and beyond state lines. The results were visible by early evening, as cars again streamed into town. By eight o'clock, they were forced to park at long distances from the Square, and the out-of-town arrivals walked to the meeting place. Here the local members of the White Crusade had already taken the choice places near the speakers' stand.

The Telford men and the constables were deployed in a thin line around Courthouse Square. Near the rostrum, a television car, surrounded by a cluster of newsmen, waited patiently as the crowd rapidly grew in size. With their professional foresight, they knew that news was coming to a boil.

The speeches began at 8:30, when Collins appeared in the bright glare of TV lights focused on him. He was feeling a heady, intoxicating triumph as he looked down upon the mass of upturned faces before him. He had willed this crowd to be here and to listen to him. He had proven himself capable of leading men in an important cause. Even the presence of Commissioner Roland at the foot of the platform, flanked by two federal marshals from Knoxville, only served to heighten his self-importance. A forewarning that he was to be re-arrested only added luster to his great moment.

"Fellow Americans!" he began. "We have come here

162

tonight to exercise our right of free speech." He spoke with a studied, ringing cadence. "No carpetbagging judge who hands out warrants for the arrest of Southern patriots, no traitorous mayor, not even the President of the United States can take away the rights of free men. No man can take away the right of Tennessee to live by its sovereign laws, which time and experience have proven durable and just. We will defend that right with our lives, if necessary." He was tuning up, and as his tempo quickened, he flayed the air with his long arms. "There will be no surrender to the turncoats," he cried, "and no knuckling under to the man who sits in Washington, working overtime to extend his greedy, federalistic grip on our free and glorious South!"

The crowd roared its approval, and the sound made Ben Collins feel dauntless.

"We are white Christians and give notice that no force on earth can mingle our blood with that of the black man," he went on. "I will read you a message sent to me tonight by Christian Baptist pastors from five states telling in words more eloquent than mine that you men and women are God's people. I quote, 'True Bible believers, North, South, East, and West, hold to the truth that God divided the races and intended them to remain so,' unquote."

"Let's shove that down the mayor's throat," Steve Prowse yelled up at him from the foot of the platform.

"Let's move into the courthouse," Jay Ford bellowed, his rehearsed words giving the impression of sudden inspiration.

Collins was silent, permitting the idea to percolate.

"Let's go into the courthouse!" echoed Drake. "We'll find the mayor hiding there."

The cry was taken up by the mob.

"Let's go!"

"What are we waiting for!"

Commissioner Roland understood Collins' purpose at once. The courthouse was the symbol of government in Jameson; the attempt to invade it could also be a ruse to upset the timetable for his arrest. Roland found it difficult to keep his hand from the sheathed gun under his coat. He was waiting nervously for the arrival of the state highway officers whom he had handpicked to aid him in the arrest. The Telford men still carried no weapons but were prepared with tear-gas guns. He gave himself another split second to see if Collins was ready to carry out his reckless plan.

To Roland's experienced eye, a premature move to take the mob's leader could set off the riot he was trying to prevent. Not to arrest him was equally dangerous. Either way, within seconds, it might be too late to prevent violence. Roland exchanged a steady look with the marshals, aware that the decision was his own to make. When he saw Collins move toward the edge of the speakers' stand, the police officer nodded. His two companions stepped forward to reach Collins as he jumped to the ground. Only those who stood close by knew what was happening. A strong-arm squad under Ford's guidance closed in to stop the arrest, and their movement caused the crowd to eddy like a wave in the direction of the platform.

A swelling siren wail suddenly pierced the air, and with it came the roar of racing motorcycles. There was a screech of braking as the state police arrived. The melee which Roland had tried to avert broke out in hand-to-hand fighting. In the uproar, no one heard Ben Collins' cry as the marshals carried him off to a waiting car.

"Remember, boys!" he shouted. "No surrender! The politicians have no guts . . . it's up to you. . . ."

The police car sped off with its motor escort toward Knoxville, as the mob, following a new leader, streamed over the lawn toward the courthouse.

Commissioner Roland shot his pistol in the air twice. It was the signal for the Telford men to use their tear-gas guns on the running crowd. One volley was enough to turn it from its objective and to send the rioters running from the acrid, blinding fumes. A second volley completed the job, and the mob was no longer capable of enough unified action to resist being swept out of the Square.

CHAPTER SIXTEEN

A SLIVER OF LIGHT came in through the slightly
opened kitchen door and fell across the floor in a sharp, thin
line. Robby lay in the wide bed in his mother's room, where
Mr. Cobb had put him with his own hands after the beating.
The bruises on his body, the puffy lips, and the throbbing of
his head were less painful now. He lay in the dark all day and
into the night, because light made his eyes ache. It had been
a long day for him, and he had time to burrow under all the
layers of his mind, examining things minutely from the inside
out. Sometimes it hurt to see things so closely, and there were
moments when he could not tell where the physical pain
ended and the ache of his spirit began.

His mother moved about quietly in the kitchen, but so

acute were his senses that he could hear everything, no matter how muffled her movements were. Mrs. Jones kept all visitors out of his room, but she had permitted Linda to stand at his bedside for a while.

At the end of the long day, he went back to blaming himself for Jerry's chickening out; for his failure to understand that the threat to bring a penknife into Fayette had been a cry for help. Everybody was afraid of white people—all the time—but Robby had not expected Jerry to be so unprepared to face them. Jerry was skulking somewhere, deeply mired in the shame of being a deserter. It was easier for Joyce Baker. She could run away with money in her pockets and set herself up in a new school.

There was little room for compassion in Robby this day, and his sympathy for Jerry was short-lived. In the first few hours after he was brought home, anger and bitterness seethed in him. But in the long run, the anger, if not the bitterness, was fruitful, for it led him to the one firm spot in his slippery, unsteady world. Before Thursday was over, Robby knew that he was going back to Fayette the next morning—on crutches if need be—and as long as there was a path open into that building, he would keep right on going and would not stop unless they killed him first.

Long after dark, his mother came into the room to tell him that Collins had been arrested and that it was quiet again in the Square. All he said when he heard the news was, "I would have gone back anyway, Mom, even if there were hundreds like him around."

Howie and Reverend Wilkins had gone to Knoxville right after the morning riot to talk to people there, and Robby wanted them to come back quickly to tell him that they would let him return to that school tomorrow. All day long the reporter's question pounded in his ears: Why do you want to go to Fayette? And all day the answers, which that white man would never understand, kept coming at him. He thought of the trip he had taken with his mother to Knoxville.

He was eleven years old then, and it was his first time out of Jameson. He hated to go, and at the same time, he couldn't put off testing himself any longer.

He just had to try moving about in their world. The sign on the Knoxville bus said the driver was safe, courteous, and reliable. He read the sign because he liked reading, while his mother paid the fare. Then they went to the back, to sit among their own people. He looked with fascination at the swiftly moving fields, at the stores and houses along the road; absorbing the strangeness as they left Jameson further behind.

The bus stopped suddenly, and the driver stood up. His hair was neatly combed, and he wore clean clothes and looked big and strong as he stood there facing the passengers, waiting for someone to get off. But no one moved, and he pointed a finger and said, "Hey you, wake up and get off!" Robby turned to look and saw that he was yelling at a Negro lady in a white dress and a white straw hat with a black ribbon around the crown. It upset Robby to see that the driver's courtesy was only for white women, though he should have known it well enough not to let the man's meanness trouble him so much. He was so upset that when they arrived in Knoxville, he made straight for the colored toilet in the station. It was awful to get caught somewhere among white people where there was no place to do it, and the fear of being caught like that made you want to get to a toilet many times. What was the use of telling a white reporter that? He couldn't tell him that getting into Fayette was like knocking a brick out of the Jim Crow wall—you got one out and it was easier to get at the rest.

Robby saw that everything Howie had ever told him made sense—like a picture puzzle when it all locked together. Howie had explained their trick of keeping colored and white children apart early enough so that the idea of being different had time to jell. Not only different (because that alone couldn't do the job), they had to make the kids with the white skin think they were *better*. But the twister on the end of the whip was the neatest trick of all. They made the Negro kids believe it too!

Robby reached slowly for the sugared water on the chair near him. His tongue felt leathery, and the sweet drink soothed it a little.

He remembered how Joel Saunders and he had rambled off on a scorching day into the Square that seemed ten times as big then as it was now. In the middle stood the round drinking fountain with the bronze-green fish spouting sparkling water from its wide open mouth. The white boy made a bee-line for it and stuck his head under the cool flow. The water gushed smack into his mouth, and Joel grinned up at him

169

happily. He had just stood there watching thirstily. Neither of them could read, but they both knew what the sign said. Joel accepted the fact that the cooling water was for whites only just as he accepted the fact of breathing.

Robby's nostrils flared and his brown eyes dilated, darting from wall to wall in the darkened, small room and back to the shadowy ceiling. Those white people who imagined he wanted to go to their school only to get an education were just plain dumb. He wanted all the rights they gave Joel Saunders or Nelson, because he was not only as good as they were—but better!

He had quite forgotten that only that morning, while his mother was soothing the welts on his body with simple remedies, he had thought of giving up the struggle and leaving school forever. Now, as his agitation started to subside, he began to see alternatives. He could make a strategic retreat back to Negro Carver, or even go up North to get an education. But no matter where his thoughts led him, all day long there were three masked faces peering at him from the landing on the stairway—the tallest of them had a pasty white face and red hair.

It was almost ten o'clock at night when Robby heard the sharp knock on the street door and his body stiffened. As soon as he recognized Reverend Wilkins' voice in the kitchen, he felt better. There was someone with the pastor, but it was not Howard Carter. Robby began to sweat at every pore as he heard an unfamiliar visitor asking his mother for permission to see him.

The narrow strip of light on the floor widened slowly, and Jacob Wilkins tiptoed in. He left the door open a small crack and sat down carefully on the edge of the bed so as not to jar him. He took Robby's hand between his own cool, bony fingers and murmured, "We heard about your getting hurt when we got to Knoxville. Our friends there got word by telephone right away. Howie stayed behind. He wants me to tell you that he's sorry he can't come to see you. We decided that he ought to remain there if we're going to need some outside help." He stroked Robby's hand gently. "I'm glad to see you, son. I can tell, even in the dark, that you look all right. Reverend Logan asked me to bring him to you. Just a little while ago, he made a speech on the radio in Knoxville and announced that if you young people want him, he is ready to walk to school with you tomorrow. But I'm afraid it will have to be without you; you'll need a little rest. Do you want him to come in here?"

Jacob Wilkins sat with his back to the kitchen light, and Robby could not see his face in the deep shadow. He hated to hurt the old man's feelings, but he didn't want the white man to come near him. He heard Logan's voice from the other room, and it made him ache in a special way—differently from the bruises on his body. But over and above the pain, Robby felt an exultant gladness that he had decided to go back before Logan's offer of help.

Robby did not answer, and the minister understood the cause of his silence. He released his hand as if to give him more freedom of choice.

"It might be good for you to take a day off, son, but it would help the others if you agreed to let Reverend Logan walk with them."

"I'm going back tomorrow morning," said Robby, his anger flaring. "I made up my mind to do it before he came here. Why must we have him? Please, Reverend Wilkins, I can't talk to him now. . . ."

There was another long silence before Robby added tiredly, "I can't help feeling that way, but if you think he ought to walk with us, it's okay. I'll be ready to go, too. But I don't want to talk now."

"I'll tell him you don't feel well," the old man said, taking up his hand again. "I think it's best to have him go along tomorrow, whether you go or not."

Not until he heard the street door close on both visitors, did the muscles of Robby's body begin to relax. His mother came into the room and stood over him.

"If you're set on going," she said quietly, "you can go, but I've got to know that you're strong enough to stand on your feet. Get up, Son, I want to see how you walk."

He drew back the thin cover and raised himself slowly, while his mother stood watching, offering no help. He put his feet down on the bare floor and took the first step with care, not to stir the pain back into his head. Barefoot, he went into the kitchen, his eyes squinting at the unshaded electric bulb. He walked around the table in the center of the room, slowly at first, and as his confidence increased, his step was firmer. He had to walk slowly even then, because it was the only way to stretch the cramped space of the little kitchen.

His white pajamas were inches too short at wrists and ankles, and in the low-ceilinged room, it seemed to the watching mother that her son was like a young plant fighting for space in which to grow.

"That white preacher," she said, as she studied the boy's walk, "has love in his heart for all God's creatures. He wants to save those folks who were in the Square from bringing more shame and sin on themselves."

That night, in the long, hazy corridor between wakefulness and slumber, Robby heard Joel Saunders shout: This way Sir Black Baboon! The words were so loud and so close to his ear that he was jolted awake.

Joel was his best friend once, but the day came when they had been in separate schools for a long time; and it was like sudden lightning and thunder to hear him say: you just keep outa my yard! The tone of it was different from any spat they ever had before, and he understood that they were not friends now. He wasn't ready for it, though he should have known that the day would come.

Even the sheet with which he was covered was too hot, and Robby threw it aside. He stared into the blue-black sky framed by the small window. Unashamedly, but without self-pity, he let the tears roll down his cheeks. The tears washed out all the strain of the long day to prepare him for the walk with the white man to which he had so grudgingly agreed.

CHAPTER SEVENTEEN

D IRTY YELLOW COWARDS," Steve Prowse said in a slow growl, punctuating the words with the bang of a beer bottle in his hand, "taking the whole lousy police force of the whole lousy county to do the job."

Prowse had been drinking steadily in the Allnite Bar and Grill since the arrest of Collins and the mob's dispersal. His face was swollen and flushed. At his side sat his crony Tom Drake. Facing the two men in the cozy booth was Ford, tightly wedged in by his Alabama friends, Herb and Lee Wayland.

The two benches at the table were just long enough to squeeze in six men. The sixth in their company was young Harry Nelson, sitting at the edge of the bench near his prospective father-in-law, Drake.

"Yeah!" Harry chimed in. "They didn't have the guts to leave him in the town jail. I bet they couldn't keep him in the lockup here. Could they? That's why they dragged him off to Knoxville!"

It was three in the morning. Outside the sky was still indigo blue. The bartender, dozing on a high stool behind the counter, was awakened by the thumping of the beer bottle and wished his late customers would go home and let him sleep.

"They're cowards all right," said Ford, "and I'm going to call their bluff. I've been putting my mind to it since they threw those stink bombs at us." His face was screwed up with the effort of slowly dredging up his thoughts from the alcohol fumes. "We gotta show folks around here how to stand up like white men. I've got it all figured out. Steve . . . you and Tom know where to lay your hands on some dynamite." He leaned across the sticky table and lowered his voice. "Let's put a charge under the high school tonight . . . what d'ya say, boys?" Jay's bloodshot, shallow eyes looked from Prowse to Drake for approval. He was very pleased with himself and the murky plan which he was outlining. When he finished, he asked happily, "How's it sound?"

A jukebox that had been blaring steadily fell silent just then, and the sudden quiet created a disturbing vacuum. Harry Nelson stretched across the table to put another coin in the wall box, and no one spoke until a loud guitar filled the air.

"We can get all we want at the mine," Drake agreed, but

his face sagged and his voice was gloomy. "I got a better idea. We got to scare the coons so bad they won't try messing around with white girls. Let's put a charge at the railroad siding right near their shacks. It'll scare the daylights out of all the nigger-lovers in this town, too."

Prowse jerked his head in an affirmative nod. "I'm for that! It'll be a warning to folks who need it . . . like the mayor and his gang." He began to laugh hysterically, making a gesture of aiming an invisible bow and arrow. "It's like the Indians did when they shot close enough to take the skin offa your nose. That's going to be our first warning. . . ."

"Okay," said Ford with as much force as he could muster. "We do it your way tonight and leave the school for another time. But there's one other little thing we gotta do. Tom, you and Steve can take care of the dynamite job before daylight. Then we gotta see to holy Matt Logan bragging about how he's gonna walk them niggers to school."

Ford's two Alabama friends showed their first signs of life and nodded agreement. There was a long silence following the new proposal.

"Whadya mean?" Drake asked worriedly. Even in his drink-befuddled state, he didn't like the sound of it.

"Logan's got to be shown that his only job is to take care of his church," said Ford cheerfully. "We can handle those colored kids without his help, and I know how to convince the parson."

The voice from the jukebox cried, "Buh-buh be my turtle-dove," as the six heads bent over the table to hear Ford outline his plan. When he had finished, he leaned back comfortably.

"It's a cinch, boys," he said with excessive joviality. "It's just the thing to show that we mean business."

Prowse and Drake were both silent. It came through to Ford that his scheme had failed to ignite. "We won't hurt the parson," he urged. "We'll just talk to him with enough sign language so he can understand. My boys here are game, ain'tcha?" He turned his head from side to side to include his two shadows, who nodded in unison.

"I'll go with you!" Harry Nelson cried. "That there Logan and his rich friends think they can run this town forever, but we'll show them different."

Tom Drake stared at his future son-in-law and was about to say something to him but changed his mind. Instead, he told Ford, "I'll do the dynamite job with Steve, but you'll have to take care of the other thing without me. I gotta turn in when we finish. Nellie'll worry if I don't get home soon." He was lying glibly, ashamed to reveal his superstitious fear of the plan. "You all can take care of Logan without me."

"Count me out, too," said Prowse briefly. "I can't make a night of it."

"I'll go, Jay!" Harry repeated with greater eagerness than before.

"Well, I guess we can handle it without you two," Ford said good-humoredly, accepting the fact that the two men would not be budged. "Harry can make up for both of you. Daylight will be busting out," he added with a spurt of energy. "Get going if you're going. I'll stand for the drinks."

Tom Drake got into Prowse's Chevy without a word, and the two were silent as they sped along the deserted road. The mine was only ten miles away, and if they wasted no time, their task could be accomplished well before daybreak. The dark fields streaked by, and they remained lost in their private drunken fancies until an interstate truck zoomed by with a roar, the blast of air shaking them both out of their torpor.

"I hope Logan gets his," Prowse mumbled, his eyes focusing waveringly on the road ahead. "If it wasn't courting bad luck, I'd be right there with those boys."

"He'll get what's coming to him," Tom prophesied malevolently. "I'm glad that kid Harry has red blood in him. I was going to stop him, but I want him to show the stuff he's made of."

When they reached the coal mine, the car stopped at a distance from the high, barred gate, and the two men found their way to a torn opening in the linked-metal fence. They broke their way into a padlocked storeroom, and Steve rapidly filled his arms with explosives from a neatly stacked pile, while Tom helped himself to the coils of fuse. Within minutes, they were in the car again and on their way back into town.

The sky was almost cloudless, still dark, and spangled with stars when they arrived at the railroad siding in Jameson. They parked the car on a dirt road. Carrying their burden, they made a path through a field of dry stubble. Insect noises sounded in the night, fireflies scattered their light in wild disorder, and in a nearby swamp, bullfrogs croaked.

"I'd like to be putting this load of firecrackers right over there in niggertown instead of on the tracks," whispered Prowse hoarsely, staring venomously in the direction of Mount Olive, whose shacks loomed in a huddled silhouette against the sky. Not a light was to be seen in the Negro quarter. A dog barked, and the cry seemed to be taken up by the canine population for miles around. The two men stopped short and waited nervously until the barking and the baying faded away. In that interval of waiting, Prowse's idea of advancing closer into Mount Olive also faded. Reassured that the dogs were nowhere near, they made the rest of the distance at a run. When they reached the tracks, Drake quickly dug a hole in the gravel roadbed, into which Prowse set the dynamite sticks. The fuse was linked, and Tom, his hands trembling with excitement, announced, "Okay, let's beat it!"

Together they uncoiled the long, carrier fuse as they made their way to the car. Winded and puffing, Prowse lit the match and waited with fascination as the splutter of greenish flame crawled snakelike along the ground, straight for the heap of explosives.

"We gotta wait and see the fireworks," he said. "I wanta see what happens to those darkies when it goes off. They're gonna hear it and start running like mad . . . scared . . . here it comes!"

The dynamite went off with a roar and a blinding light that burst apart into cascading illuminations. The scooped-out earth and splintered wooden railroad ties rose high from their crater. In the eerie flash, the ground shook under the feet of the watching men. When it was over, Prowse stared open-mouthed. Not a glimmer of light appeared anywhere. The meaning of the darkness was not wasted on the dynamiters. It told them that Mount Olive gave notice that they were not sitting ducks for the potshots of white night riders.

Prowse swore a long string of expletives.

"I bet they even got guns in there," said Tom Drake. "We'll show them next time. Come on, let's go."

A rooster crowed as they got into the car and drove away. In the east, the darkness and the stars were fading out of the sky.

CHAPTER EIGHTEEN

Mrs. JONES said she was going with him to
the top of the hill to meet the white minister, and Robby did
not protest. When they left the shack at eight o'clock, there
were neighbors standing around to wave good-bye. A man
with sleep still in his eyes, barefoot, and wearing a rumpled
slept-in T-shirt called out to him, "You look mighty good this
morning, boy!"

Robby grinned back with embarrassment, aware of the
generous sympathy. "I feel pretty good, Mr. Abernathy, thank
you." He lowered his eyes to avoid other such encounters.

Down the road they met Linda, escorted by the four
younger Tilsons, two boys and two girls, who surrounded
Robby noisily yelling, "What did they do to you?"

181

Linda tried to silence them, while she herself studied him closely.

"You all right?" she asked quietly.

"Do I look sick?" The words were prickly with annoyance, but when he saw the confusion in her eyes, he became contrite.

"I'm okay. I feel so good I can hardly believe it." He said it loudly for the small fry to hear. "I got ambushed." He made further amends, adding with pantomime, "They went ra-ta-ta, but their aim was bad."

Along the road they picked up Claudia, Bettylou, Ellen, Amos, and a few parents. Together they made a slow, quiet procession, becoming completely silent as they approached the meeting place.

Jerry Moore's absence hung over Robby like a haunt; he hadn't shown his face since the Wednesday meeting. No one knew how he killed time. Joyce was in faraway New York, but her abdication, though a blot on them all, was a lot easier to bear. Jerry couldn't run far like Simon Baker's daughter; he had to stay and face his defeat.

Reverend Logan was at the top of the hill awaiting them, and Robby could see his large silhouette looming against the bright morning sky. There was another white man with him whose unheralded appearance made Robby stiffen with apprehension, then grow hot with resentment.

Jacob Wilkins was with the two men, ready to smooth the rough edges of the encounter. He explained the presence of the stranger. The little man with round shoulders was Mr.

Brown, a bookkeeper at the hosiery mill in town. With excitement in his voice, Reverend Wilkins told the assembled group that until today they had not known each other. When Brown heard the radio broadcast which told of Logan's mission, he had immediately driven to the parsonage at Crestwood and asked to be taken along.

Robby limply shook the extended hand of the tall, hatless man in clerical garb, and then the hand of the other white man. His face was without expression as his lax fingers were held in the alien clasps.

When the six students had been introduced, the white minister stood towering above them as though he were installed in a pulpit. But it was his whiteness, not his size, and not the aura of his calling, which compelled Robby to listen as Logan declared that the pre-dawn explosion on the doorstep of the Negro district would awaken the people of Jameson to the danger of its passive acceptance of injustice and evil. He told in detail of the steps taken to provide full security for the six students within the school building—even to having monitors accompany them to washrooms; and he assured them of safe conduct home.

"Mr. Brown and I are not alone in seeking salvation in brotherly love," he said, and his eyes were filled with sadness as he added, "many strive for this goal, but few achieve it. Those who find their way are indeed among the blessed. Mr. Brown and I have come here to begin atonement for our sins by sharing your burden, and we give thanks to the Lord for the privilege of walking with the students this morning."

Robby heard him out but made no effort to meet him even halfway in understanding the full meaning of the words. Why these two had come was their business. They could not take away the smallest fraction of his victory. He had chosen to go back to Fayette before their proffered aid. It was a triumph which filled him with a bitter joy.

It was time to go. Robby exchanged good-bye glances with his mother. He felt Reverend Logan's light touch on his arm.

"You and I will walk in front," the minister said, with a slight smile, but his eyes remained sad. "Brown will bring up the rear."

When they reached Main Street, Robby could see the outline of a mob filling the road near the high school and heard their voices muffled by distance. But almost at once, they encountered the helmeted auxiliary police widely spaced along their path. Collins' arrest had in no way checked the well-oiled machine he had set in motion; the turnout was even larger than yesterday. At every step, the chanting grew louder:

KEEP NIGGERS OUT!   KEEP NIGGERS OUT!

The principal of Fayette High stood at the central doors awaiting them; his usual boyish look was completely erased, and he was haggard and hollow-eyed as he watched Matthew Logan's steady progress toward him. His customary steady nerves were beyond control as he heard the cries of the mob reach toward ever higher levels of obscenity. In the face of the hysterical bawling, Cobb almost felt a grudging respect for the man who walked at the head of the Negro children.

He wondered for the first time since the trouble began, if he had been wrong to regard Matthew as a sinister conspirator. Perhaps he was only a foolish man whose religious zeal deprived him of ordinary reasonableness.

Cobb was still under the softening influence of the hope that Logan's folly was no more than a temporary aberration, when the six children arrived at the entrance and his unhappy eyes met the minister's with uncertainty.

"Well, you've done your part," he said. "Now take care of yourself."

His words were drowned out in the earsplitting din which arose as the Negro students entered the building.

The pastor sighed with relief as the doors closed, and he and George Brown turned their backs on the school. Logan stared squarely at the crowd in front of him, held there in check below the sidewalk. His heart sank as he saw the faces in the mob for the first time this morning. Pity for them, and for all of Jameson, overwhelmed him.

As he reached the sidewalk, a young matron carrying a handbag on a long brassy chain broke the police cordon and swung it swiftly at the minister.

"Nigger-lover!" she screamed. "You're a devil in disguise!"

Logan stood transfixed as he looked into her tortured eyes. The woman was pushed roughly back into the crowd, and a police officer urged him to continue on his way.

At Chestnut Street, Logan and Brown shook hands, their paths separating. The minister began his solitary walk along the tree shaded, deserted street which rose gradually into the hills of Crestwood and the parsonage. He was unable to shake off the woman's hate-twisted face.

If this woman had children of her own, he thought, they were already tainted and debased by the same sickness. He suddenly despaired of ever being able to do enough to help such people become purged of this self-destroying poison.

Logan was so preoccupied with his thoughts that when a figure darted out from behind the broad trunk of a tree and stood before him, he could only look up vacantly. Simultaneously his arms were clutched from behind. He could have freed himself then because he was a strong man, yet he remained inert. There was a sharp jab at his stomach which doubled him over. Fists struck him from all sides, but he did nothing to protect himself. Before he could recover the will to fight back, he was struck a telling blow that knocked him to the ground. Logan's head struck the jagged circle of stones bordering the earth under a huge elm. He lay on his back in the shadow of the tree. The sun filtering through the leaves made a mottled tracery upon his upturned face. One of his attackers directed a final kick at his unconscious figure, and there was a crunching sound as a heavy shoe struck an eye socket.

A screen door opened on a porch, and a woman appeared in time to see the last vicious blow before the assailants fled. The door banged loudly as she ran down the steps.

"Oh, Lord, have mercy!" the woman wailed.

The four assailants were out of sight before she reached the prone man on the sidewalk.

CHAPTER NINETEEN

T HAT EVENING Robby left home after supper with only one thought—to be alone—beyond the confines of the Negro district and its inhabitants. The darkness itself was a protection against people. He kicked angrily at a tin can in the road and watched its glinting flight through the moonlight until it landed.

Dull anger nibbled at him, searching for the cause into which it could sink its teeth. The thought of the white man lying in a bed in Phelps Hospital only served to remind him that because of Logan, the doors of Fayette were closed now to both black and white. The principal had announced in an emergency assembly that they would remain shut until Washington agreed to send troops to assure law and order.

Jerry Moore had crawled out of his hole to gloat that the school was going to stay shut forever, rather than let colored kids in, and they would all have to go back to Carver with their tails between their legs.

Robby echoed the prediction as his own, accepting and embellishing it darkly with the weight of his own dejection. He was going back to Carver, and he was minus his job and would never get another one as good while he was in high school. Fayette was closed, and he was nowhere at all. He clung to his anger rather than face that great emptiness in him. Gone was the morning's elation when he was ready to face lions in the way. Wrathfully he told himself that he never really believed he would get an education in that white school; not for a single minute since he had walked the first gauntlet of jeers and insults. He had just let himself pretend, knowing all the time he wouldn't get a diploma in that school.

His thoughts returned to Logan, and it was like reading about a catastrophe that happened far away to a man whom he did not know. There was no cord of sympathy connecting him to that white man. Yet try as he might, he could not forget him. The attack on Logan bound them together, no matter what happened from now on. Even if they sent troops into town, it would be only because the palefaces of Jameson were afraid that the mob was a danger to their own skins.

Robby's eyes looked up the winding dirt road. His feet and the tin can had taken him into Barrow Lane, and he saw the lighted windows and open doorway of the Tilsons' home. It was a two-room shack with a wavy, thin-roofed porch through which the moon shed its light. Linda sat on a porch step surrounded by her brothers and sisters. He realized the moment he saw her that she was the only person he could bear to be with tonight. She jumped up and ran toward him, bringing the children along like a magnet.

They were shaken off finally, and the boy and girl left Barrow Lane behind. They walked in silence. The straggle of shacks dropped away until there was nothing but the wasteland of stunted pine and the tall weeds and rock outcroppings which lay behind Mount Olive. They walked close together, and the harsh ugliness of the land, baked brittle by the sun, so ugly by day, was for them washed smooth and soft by the moonlight. They walked without touching, until they found a boulder large enough to provide a backrest where they could sit side by side.

The anger in Robby had gradually left him, and in its place was a slowly spreading balm and gladness such as he had never felt before in his life. There were times when he had known great happiness in just lying on his back on the ground, looking at an afternoon sky where shining cloud cities were peopled with the life of his own imagining. What he felt now resembled that stirring joy, but the present moment was far better because Linda was at his side.

The rock against which he rested was still warm from the day-long sun. Robby breathed deeply of the sweet scent in the air and listened with uplifted face to the symphony of invisible night insects. It was a long time since he had tried to unravel these sounds. The buzz of the grasshoppers was like a muted soft-shoe dance; the crickets trilled in short bursts of music, and he was able to single out the rhythm of the cicada as it began a low scissor-grinder buzz, rising louder all the time. Robby looked at the benign-faced moon in the almost cloudless sky and marveled at the happiness of having someone like Linda at his side to share it.

When he turned his gaze from the moon and stared into her face, he looked in wonder at the beauty of her serious eyes and the graceful shape of her head leaning against the rock. She was so beautiful that his heart began to pound. He turned away, and everywhere he looked there was new beauty to behold. Even the rocks in the field, the scrubby trees and weeds and grasses were beautiful in the moonlight.

The touch of Linda's shoulder against his own was a new sensation. Love had dropped a soft curtain between Robby and the harsh world, and he was very happy. His bitterness was gone, and with his hope renewed he could believe in the future again. Even that insistent, ugly memory of Linda sprawled on the corridor floor of Fayette seemed less painful tonight. Robby had fought the white boys with passivity, he remembered, not with violence but with self-control. It was *he* who had fought for and won his own self-respect.

"Hey! Woman," he blurted out with a smile, "maybe you better forget about being a teacher. How about taking up nursing and working for me when I'm a doc? How about that?"

The smile that lit up his eyes made Linda think that she had never seen anyone so handsome. She laughed with delight and shook her head and laughed still more, knowing that she ought to be nodding assent instead.

Robby let himself be carried away by his imagination. "It'll be a good job. You'll sit in a nice office in a big place like Knoxville. I'll get me running hot and cold water, an electric refrigerator and a gas stove for Mom. No more wood fires for the Jones family. I'll also get me a wife, I think. If anybody will have me, that is."

"You won't have trouble finding a wife, I expect." The laughter almost faded from her face as Linda added, "Joyce Baker would come back running, if you asked her." She felt the firm muscles of Robby's arm through the thin sleeve of her dress and wished he would encircle her shoulder so that she could lean her cheek against his. Joyce knew how to manage such things better, she thought enviously, but she could not bring herself to the point of taking the first step.

Suddenly Robby's arm reached around her. His warm lips touched her cheek as she leaned against him. Their lips met as she lifted her face, and he enclosed her in an embrace so tight that she could not breathe. When he relaxed his hold, she sighed with contentment. They sat without talking, savoring the wonderful moment of having found each other.

Linda ran her fingers tenderly over Robby's cheek, letting her touch tell him of her love far better than words.

"You know," she murmured, "I'm glad they closed that school. I don't want you to get hurt again."

The moment it was said, she knew with dismay that her words had shattered their private world of joy just as if it were made of glass and she had thrown the stone. It was dumb to remind him of what had happened and of what still lay ahead. She could feel at once that Robby had left her to go back to the frightening world outside.

"I don't mean that," she said bleakly. "I really want Fayette to open on Monday! What I meant was it's terrible to have it closed after all we had to go through, especially you, Robby. I wouldn't want to see all that wasted. . . . It would be awful!" She had spoken the truth but knew it wouldn't help. Yet she went on, trying to repair what couldn't be mended. "They'll open Fayette soon, but any way it turns out, you can still be a doctor. We've got Carver to go back to."

"Zatso? I'm not going into that crummy high school again!" Robby exploded, drawing his knees up under his chin. "A little while ago I was ready to do that, but now I'm not so sure I want to go to any school around here. You might as well know what I really think. They're not going to let us into Fayette again. They shut the school just to keep us out. Jerry is on your side," he added, trying to wound her. "He's also glad the way things turned out, because now he doesn't have to feel rotten any more about chickening out. Why should I care if we don't go back to their lousy white school? I won't stop living any more than he did."

"But you can't compare yourself to Jerry Moore," she protested quietly, "not after what you did."

All happiness had fled from Linda too, because Robby would not accept the proffered comfort she yearned to give him. They were both silent and though it was difficult to leave the magic spot where they had known brief joy, Robby jumped to his feet and held out his hand.

"Let's go back," he said, keeping his eyes from her.

They took the path back to Barrow Lane, and he felt Linda's fingers slide into his hand. He gripped them tightly, like someone holding to a steadying prop where the ground was uncertain.

"How they must hate us," Robby murmured almost to himself . . . "to stomp one of their own . . . a minister . . . and I hate every one of them, too. And please, Linda!" he added with passion. "Don't try to make me out to be better than Jerry or anybody else. Because I don't know what I am!"

There was an uninvited guest in the Jones's kitchen when Robby got home. Joyce Baker's father was seated at the lino-leum-covered table. The back of his head, which merged with his glistening fat neck, resembled a seal. His agitated fleshy face was covered with a film of perspiration. In front of him lay the spotless, wide felt hat which he wore summer and winter. Its costly appearance reminded Robby that Mount Olive people laughed behind this rich man's back, saying that he tried to ape the white banker Oglethorpe's headgear.

"Mr. Baker has been waiting a long time for you, Son," Louella Jones said.

"That's right, boy," echoed the visitor fretfully. "I want to talk to you." His impatience did not permit him to wait for Robby to sit down. "I guess you can see now that my advice was good right along. They're never going to open that

193

school to colored kids, just like what happened in Virginia. But that's not the worst they can do. Jameson has always been a fine place for us. We never had trouble here, and you just don't know how good you've got it, boy! If you lived in some other places I know, you'd understand what I mean. But all that got changed when Carter and Wilkins and their Association friends started this crazy business. Especially Howard Carter with his Communistic talk!"

Baker leaned across the table to where Robby sat and leveled a pudgy forefinger at his face. "But I fixed him! He'll never get a job in this town again."

Robby's mouth hung open as he heard Baker's unabashed admission that he made Howie lose his job. He should have known right away; who else but Baker would have dared to stool? Robby lowered his eyes quickly to hide his anger and disgust.

"I tell you we're in real trouble now," Simon Baker went on stridently, oblivious to the effect of his words. "If they whipped Logan, they're ready to do a lot worse to some colored people I can think of. Those soldiers they talk about—if they get here—won't be on our side; you know that. That Barlow woman and the mayor and the rest of that crowd are going to run for cover like rabbits and leave us in the lurch now that they got everything boiling up around here. As for your friend Howie, he isn't around, and if he does come back it won't be to stay. He knows it's too hot for him in Jameson."

Robby's teeth ground shut. He didn't dare call Baker a rat and a liar to his face. He wished he knew what the man was driving at and sought his mother's eyes for a clue. But in them he found only an unnerving, empty neutrality. He knew there wasn't a word of truth in what the man was saying—except about Fayette staying closed. Maybe Mount Olive was good enough for Simon Baker, but not for anybody else. The fat snake knew that everybody who lived here was scabby poor. The elementary school was a one-room, tar-paper hut with a leaky roof, and Carver was a chicken coop compared to the white high school. The sneak was also wrong about Howie . . . he was coming back home all right. Robby could bet on it.

"It's up to you!" Baker screamed at him. "You can stop murder here! Tell Jacob Wilkins you ain't going along with him and his troublemaking northern friends any more. If you and your mother pull out of it, the others will go along." His high-pitched voice dropped abruptly and became wheedling. "I came here with a good proposition for you. I told your mother, and now I'm going to lay it out for you—I know you want to be a doctor. Maybe you're trying to fly too high for a poor colored boy—I'm not saying yes or no; and I'm ready to help you, if you go back to Carver. I'll help you get through high school and give you a hand when you're ready for Fisk or Howard. I'll see that you have a good job when you need it. But you've got to give up this Fayette craziness this minute and go back to Carver on your own Monday morning. I could even think of giving you a hand, if you came to me and said you want to go up North like Joyce did."

Baker's voice dropped. "I got something to tell you about

Joyce. She doesn't want any of you kids to hear about it, but I can trust you to keep a secret. You know why she listened to reason? And her mother, too!

"On Wednesday afternoon, they did something to my girl in that school." His voice fell even lower. "She was in the washroom combing her hair in front of the mirror there—you know Joyce has pretty hair—and four white girls grabbed her, and they got two boys to help, and they stuck her head into a toilet bowl. They couldn't have done it without the boys. She fought hard, but they stuck her head in."

Robby's staring eyes flew to his mother again. This time her face told him that it was true.

Baker's voice suddenly turned buttery and wheedling again. "We want everything quiet around her—the way it always was—don't we, boy? You're smart, and if you get a good education, you might be a rich doctor some day. What do you say to my offer?" His heavy body seemed to relax, as though his proposal was unassailable. "Your mother will be proud of you when you're a doctor. She says she leaves it up to you to decide."

The only sound in the kitchen was that of Mrs. Jones stirring in the creaky chair, while Robby tried to absorb all the shocks.

"You don't have to make up your mind right away, Son," his mother said. "Mr. Baker can wait for your answer if you need time to think it over."

"Why not now?" Baker shouted. "Remember, that offer is good only until tomorrow night. I've got to know by early

Sunday morning where you stand." He turned angrily upon Louella Jones. "He could make up his mind tonight if you told him to. Don't forget that I went to a colored school, and I'm doing all right. White folks treat us fine here—don't you forget that either!"

Mrs. Jones's answer was to stand up, putting an end to Baker's visit. Robby was glad that she had practically taken the matter out of his own hands. He could not have given a direct answer even if he tried.

"Mom's right, Mr. Baker," he muttered. "I've got to think it over."

There was nothing else for Baker to do but leave. When the door closed on him and Robby was certain that he had really gone away, he exploded hotly, "He's a snake, Mom! Some day I'd like to pay him off for making Howie lose his job. He knows Howie can't do anything about it when he finds out."

The tightly stretched control which he had had over himself all day snapped suddenly as he screamed, "Gosh, everybody is stinking rotten. I wish I really had the money to go away. I can't go back to Carver; and even if Fayette opened and let me in, I don't know if I could stick it out. Baker is a rat, but I ought to take his lousy money—it's about the only time he'd ever give any of it away—and I'd get out of here! You know he's right about one thing. They may not let us go back to Fayette after what happened."

Mrs. Jones saw the strain on his face and let him talk himself out.

"Well? Why don't you say something?" he demanded of her. "You heard him say he would help me through high school if I went up North. What do you think about that, Mom?"

"How much help did Mr. Baker say he would give you?" she asked gently. "I don't exactly recollect, Son."

"What difference does that make? I'm asking you what you think of the idea? Suppose they fix it so I can't get into Fayette. I'd be passing up a chance to go to a good school somewhere else."

His mother nodded. "You may be right, Robby. We must look at every side of it. It's going to be a hard pull for you to get a doctor's education—it's almost impossible for a poor white boy, and it's going to be even harder for us, with both working all the time. It isn't as though you had a father or brothers and sisters to help." She sat down again, heavily, avoiding Robby's tense, concentrated look. "Things have been coming to a head fast. As soon as I heard that they hurt the preacher, I said to myself, this is where the white folks must make up their minds about what has to be done."

Mrs. Jones raised her eyes to Robby's. "It's only fair to talk over Baker's offer with Reverend Wilkins before you decide anything. We can see him together tomorrow night at choir practice, when I come back from work. You'll know better by then what you want to do. There'll still be time to give Baker his answer. Maybe Carter will be back soon, and you'll want to talk with him, too."

For a moment Robby felt an angry suspicion that his

mother had avoided committing herself to anything. But she gave him no opportunity to protest.

"It's late, Son, and I'm very tired. This was a terrible day for us all when they hurt that man of God. We can't talk about it any more tonight." She mollified him completely when she added, "What I think about Baker isn't as important as what you decide to do. Whichever way you choose, it will have to do. And there's time enough tomorrow."

Her words acted on Robby as though a valve had suddenly been opened and all the pressure of disappointment, anger, and frustration which had built up in him to the breaking point had suddenly lost all its force.

"I'm tired, too," he said, his body slumping. He wanted nothing so much at this moment as to forget about everything except Linda. He ached to be by himself, to go back to the newly discovered oasis which he had found with her—beyond which all that was ugly and painful in the world did not exist.

Robby was glad when his mother went into her own room, leaving him alone in the kitchen. He made up his bed quickly and put out the light, undressing in the dark. He lay with his hands under his head and stared into the night through the uncurtained window. The sky was bright with moonlight, and Robby remembered only the joy of being near Linda. He did not yet understand that this was love; he only knew that when he thought of her, all pain and misery was blotted out and he was happy.

CHAPTER TWENTY

W HEN ROBBY AWAKENED the next morning,
he struggled to keep his mind a blank. Not until he heard the
first sound of movement in his mother's room, did he become
tense and wide awake. Long before his mind told him he had
nothing to get up for, his body responded to habit, and he was
ready to jump out of bed. But instead, he extended his long
limbs spread-eagle fashion on the narrow cot. Unlike other
mornings, the stretch was not to draw out the last luxurious
moment of rest but to grasp at something for the empty day
ahead.

His mind flew to Linda, but even this consolation was
beyond reach. She worked every Saturday, hiring herself out
to scrub and iron and take care of babies, and he would not

be able to see her all day. Robby's attention was caught by a monster-sized fly buzzing loudly against the window screen over his bed. Any other time, he would have grabbed a wad of paper to swat it, but this morning he watched its jerky movements with inertia, while his mind dwelt on the strangeness of not going to a job. For the first time in three years, he was free on a Saturday, but the prospect of a day of idleness was no more pleasant to contemplate than if he were being kept home under lock and key.

When he heard his mother dressing, he threw off his thin blanket and jumped out of bed. He folded the cot out of the way and quickly got into workday clothes. Robby helped prepare breakfast with a clatter of activity. When Mrs. Jones finally went off to her job, he immediately tore into his chores just as if he had very urgent business waiting for him after the household tasks.

The spurt of energy carried him steadily through all of his responsibilities. Only then did he give out like a punctured balloon. He collapsed into the wicker chair near the radio and flicked the dial. It was the only station he ever used, and it blasted and blared love songs all day long. The kitchen was filled with twanging guitars, drums, and horns accompanying the songs of happy lovers, or just as often their sorrows.

But the radio did not shut out Robby's thoughts. He had no further excuse to put off the pressing business he had to settle for himself. He was facing himself now, unwillingly, and he knew in the bright light of day that it was one thing to tell Linda or his mother that he wanted to go away, far away, to a place where there were no Harry Nelsons; but it was another matter to tell Reverend Wilkins or Howie the same thing.

The little clock standing on the iron ledge of the stove continued to tick off the minutes when the disc jockey interrupted the music to peddle soaps, cigarettes, and medicine. Hourly, with a regularity which the boy awaited with increasing concern, the announcer delivered a bulletin on the progress of Reverend Logan. Try as he might, Robby could not help thinking of Logan and Fayette, for neither bebop nor jazz could drown out the fact that he did not want to give up his schooling. If he couldn't go to Fayette or to Carver, there was still Baker's offer. He could give up and go up North like thousands of other colored people.

As the day moved toward evening, and his idleness lay heavily upon him, his thoughts ranged uncontrolled; they were like a team of horses pulling in opposite directions, without a driver in command, getting him nowhere.

When his mother came home from work, they ate the simple meal which he had prepared, and their supper passed almost in silence. Mrs. Jones praised the hamburger and said the coffee was very good. She told him how grateful they must all be that surgery had saved one of Reverend Logan's eyes. Robby waited impatiently for her to say something about their meeting with Jacob Wilkins, but she seemed to act as though Simon Baker's visit had never taken place.

When supper was over, she said, "You've had a long holiday, Son. Tonight you can do all the tidying up while I take a little rest. Then I'll change my clothes, and we'll find out what's to be done about Fayette."

Robby was angered to speechlessness. She had forgotten that he, too, had something to say about what he was going to do! But she was already in her room, with the door shut between them, when he found his tongue.

"I don't care what anybody thinks," he cried. "I can't go back to school around here no matter what happens! Mom, do you hear?"

"I know how you feel, Son," she replied through the thin door. "Did you forget what I said last night? Anything you decide will be all right."

The Mount Olive choir met on Saturday night. After the week's scrubbing, cooking, fetching, and digging for white folks, it came none too soon to heal the ragged edges of the soul. It was a time for Mrs. Jones to reaffirm her dignity as a householder, a parent, and a respected member of a community—a right denied her as soon as she left the settlement for work outside. Choir practice was also a chance to gossip and to argue over public affairs. Neither Louella Jones nor any other member ever skipped the event except in time of illness or other misfortune.

This Saturday night the singing would have to come later in the evening, giving precedence to the unscheduled, but more important school meeting. When Robby arrived with his mother, he slunk into a chair in the shadowy corner near the entrance, while Mrs. Jones took her place near the battered old piano where the choir gathered. Scanning the assembly for a glimpse of Linda, Robby found her sitting with the rest of the Tilson family. The wish to be near her became mixed with relief at having the barrier of chairs between them, providing him with a reprieve from her questioning eyes. His roving gaze failed to locate Howie in the crowded church, and he moodily shrugged off his absence. Facing the audience was the NAACP representative from Knoxville, a spruce young lawyer.

Robby saw Reverend Wilkins and his mother with their heads bent in conversation, and an anxious suspicion seized him that she was jumping the gun. The next thing he might hear would be Wilkins making Baker's offer public. Cursing Simon Baker, Robby wished he had stayed home and left it to his mother to tell the old man anything she chose. He shrank from facing Wilkins while he still felt so uncertain. These harried thoughts were interrupted by a sharp nudge in his ribs.

"Am I right, Robby?" a middle-aged woman sitting next to him asked. "The choir *will* sing in the white church come Christmas time!"

He was caught in the dispute between Mrs. Wilson, his mother's friend, and the adversary, the man who leaned across him. "I don't know. . ." Robby began lamely.

The opposition cut in, "It's all the same to me. I don't see where singing brings us any closer to jubilee."

"There's many who don't agree with you," Mrs. Wilson reproved him briskly, "especially Robby's mother. Isn't that the truth, boy?"

"I guess so," he answered absently, his eyes on Reverend Wilkins, who was still bending an ear.

The choirmaster opened the meeting and put an end to the confab. He was a thin, springy man with a light complexion and a dark moustache no wider than an eyebrow. With his usual ebullience—as though neither flood nor fire could lessen the importance of his music—he invited everyone present to remain after the school meeting and join in the singing.

Then Reverend Wilkins came to the lectern. "Let us stand and pray, brothers and sisters," he said. He clasped his hands together and lowered his head.

When silence came, he intoned: "We meet here tonight to thank Thee, O Lord, for Thy mercy in preserving the sight of Matthew Logan, a mortal man who has taken the lonesome road once followed by a poor carpenter. We pray that he be quickly restored in health and returned to his flock.

"We pray, O Lord, that Matthew Logan, who set forth to instill in his brethren the miracle of love shall have his labors crowned with the fruit of Thy beneficence.

"We pray that the day will come when all men shall invoke Thy name; when all who dwell on earth, created in Thy image, recognize that they are brethren."

Alone among all the bowed heads, Robby's head was thrown back as though to catch every word.

"Hasten the day," the minister prayed, "that iniquity is made dumb and wickedness vanishes like smoke; and for the dominion of arrogance to pass away from the earth.

"Give us strength, O God, to continue on the path of righteousness, which alone can lead us as brethren—one in spirit and one in fellowship, forever united before Thee. Then shall Thy kingdom be established on earth. May we find strength to meet adversity with quiet courage and unshaken trust. Weeping may tarry for the night, but joy cometh in the morning. Help us to understand that injustice and hate will not forever afflict the sons of man; that righteousness and mercy will triumph in the end. Amen."

Robby had never listened so carefully from first to last, so single-mindedly to a prayer, and a voice within him cried passionately: that promise was going to come true—he might be dead and gone by then—but some day it would be like that! Forgotten for the moment was his own rancor; bitterness was shorn of its power over him. Once again he felt himself stirred deeply by the purpose of his people, in whose cause he was swept along.

When the prayer ended, Reverend Wilkins called upon the lawyer to speak, but before he had time to say more than a dozen words, there was a loud creak of footsteps on the bare wooden floor. Robby turned his head and saw white people standing in the doorway. Mr. Cobb was in the lead, and behind him were three young people. One was Mrs. Barlow's daughter, Jane; the other two were Andrew Sinclair and Joel Saunders.

Reverend Wilkins greeted the visitors across the length of the church as though the arrival of white people was an ordinary event. Yet it was so quiet that the only sound Robby heard was his own breathing and the creak of the floor, as he followed Joel's progress down the aisle. He watched him waiting awkwardly, while Mr. Cobb spoke with Reverend Wilkins and the lawyer. When their talk was over, Mr. Cobb remained standing, but places were made in the front row for his three young companions.

Reverend Wilkins, whose face seemed to be shining with some happy discovery, announced abruptly, "Our guests came here to talk to Robby Jones. But Mr. Cobb, the principal of Fayette High School, has good news for everyone."

Cobb's gravity was striking, as he began to speak, "We came to look for Jones, but now that we are here I have something to report to all of you."

He declared that the mayor had officially asked the Justice Department in Washington to place Jameson under federal protection.

"I promise you," he said with emotion, "that no mob will ever take over Jameson. It doesn't matter who they are or where they come from; they cannot destroy law and order here. Nobody is happy about having outsiders do the work for us which we ought to be doing ourselves, but the presence of federal troops will convince the lawless elements that we mean to stand by our civic trust. Tonight we start a ten o'clock curfew in Jameson and a road block to turn back out-of-town cars that have no legitimate business here.

"If the mayor's request is met and we get federal help before Monday morning, Fayette High School will open its doors at the usual time. We agreed to accept eight students, and we will keep that promise. The leaders of this town have taken matters into their own hands again. We have never had trouble between the races here, because we have no extremists on either side. We intend to keep it that way."

He left for the last that which touched him most deeply. He spoke a few words of sympathy for Matthew Logan but dwelt at length on how profoundly the attack on the Crestwood minister had shocked the townspeople and galvanized them into action. Overnight everything had changed.

"Most of the parents," he said, "understand now that it was wrong to keep their children out of school. The P.T.A., the student council, civic organizations, and churches are all ready to help bring the absentees back when Fayette opens. Those who took part in the cowardly assault are in jail and will get their due punishment. The two men who dynamited the tracks are locked up in Knoxville, and Jay Ford's Klan friends have all gone back to Alabama in a great hurry."

For the first time since he came into the church, Cobb's somber face cleared as he turned to his young companions.

"Now we can go on with the business which brought us to Mount Olive," he said. "Andrew Sinclair, the president of our student council, will tell you about it."

Robby had not taken his eyes from Cobb, and his feeling of self-consciousness had become intolerable.

Young Sinclair faced the audience without any sign of nervousness. He spoke with ease and told of last night's hurriedly called meeting of the student council at the home of Mrs. Barlow.

"I know we could have done more to help the Carver students feel at home in Fayette," he said. "We could have done something on Monday to stop things from getting worse, when we saw there were kids all set to make trouble. But we didn't; that's because we thought we were doing enough by *not* being one of the troublemakers. And that's just what got us all in trouble!"

In a burst of speed, he added, "It was after what they did to Reverend Logan that we really got shook up. We decided to do something without wating for the grown-ups to tell us what to do. All of our council members and our friends have already started telephoning and visiting parents of kids who stayed out of school. We did it on our own!" Andrew repeated the boast as he caught Jane Barlow's frantic signaling. He acknowledged her sign language with a nod and spoke faster.

"We made up a committee last night to visit Robby Jones. Jane Barlow and Saunders volunteered. Joel Saunders isn't on the student council, but he came to our meeting and asked us to take him along. We came to tell Jones that most of the Fayette students are ashamed of what happened to him and to the others from Carver High. We want to apologize for the bad time they had and to promise that we will do everything to help make things easier for them when our school opens again. It was Mrs. Barlow's idea to ask our principal to come with us to Jones's home. When we got there. . . ."

For the second time that evening there was a turning of heads, and the creak of chairs was loud enough to drown

209

out the speaker. Robby tore his steady gaze from Sinclair to look toward the door and saw that Howie was back! Simon Baker was again proven a liar!

Andrew Sinclair impatiently picked up the threads of his speech as the new arrival sat down.

"When we got to Jones's home," he continued, "a neighbor told us that he was in church. We want to tell Jones and the other new students that we kids can get along together if you give us time—I mean, if all the parents let us try."

With the infinite kindness which Robby had learned to expect from Jacob Wilkins, the pastor let him reply as the spokesman for his group from his place. He got to his feet quickly when he was called upon, but his legs felt like jelly.

"I thank you in the name of all of us from Carver," he said in a voice that sounded strong in spite of himself. "I know we will all do our best to get along with everybody at Fayette High School." He sat down with a thud, miscalculating the distance to the chair. But he felt a greater shock at realizing that he had said he was returning to that school if those doors opened again! It was as though he had just been released from a cavern into sunlight, and he thought that all of his agonizing had been hooey from the start; he would have gone back no matter what. But the darkness had been terrible while it lasted.

The white visitors were filing out through the aisle, with Mr. Cobb again in the lead, and Robby knew why Joel was trailing so slowly. When he was only a few chairs distant their eyes met, and Joel said, "Be seeing you!"

"Hi!" Robby answered. "See you."

The NAACP lawyer, whose sentence had been broken off in the middle when the white visitors arrived, tried to begin again. But it was difficult to maintain order, and the buzz of talk continued while he spoke. Only the reappearance of the choir leader signaled that the meeting was officially over.

Everybody stayed on, even those who, like Howie, sang on a single note. Many fine voices carried the less musical along when the hymn started; together they sounded like the chords of a reverberating organ:

> *Rise and shine and shout for glory, glory,*
> *Rise and shine and shout glory, glory,*
> *Soldiers of the cross.*

Robby sang with all the stops out. His eyes met Linda's looking at him happily across the rows that separated them. Then and there, he made up his mind to tell her some day about Joel Saunders—how he couldn't get him out of his system during the crazy week that was behind him. But there was nothing left for Robby to say to Reverend Wilkins tonight. The day's solitary thinking had blown away like soft down in the wind. He remembered with surprise and a sudden glow of pride that he had kept his part of the school agreement so far; and if those white students were willing to try, he could always fulfill his share of the deal with honor.

There was an intermission when the first hymn ended, and Robby swiftly made his way to Howie's side. They pumped each other's hand as though they had been separated for years. Linda joined them and looked on silently, her face radiant.

"Did you get a job in Knoxville?" Robby asked.

"What put that into your head? I hated like anything not to come back right away, boy, but I'm glad to see those goons didn't lay you low."

"I know who squealed to Tompkins about you," Robby said in a blaze of anger. "It was Simon Baker. He told me so! He said you were never coming back here."

Howie laughed. "Baker has a cast-iron pump where his heart ought to be. If he had a real one, he'd know how hard it is for people to leave the place where they were born." His eyes were warm when he added, "I knew right away that he was the stoolie. But I figured you were taking enough dirt, so I didn't want to load more on you. I knew you'd catch on quick enough."

"How about your job," Robby persisted anxiously. "Did you find work in Knoxville?"

"Now you know that's not what I went for." Howie pretended to be miffed. "I wasn't planning to throw in the sponge. I was just sitting on the tail of our people there to needle them about getting Washington to do something. Don't worry about me," he said. "They need a cleanup man at the *Courier* print-shop, and I can get the job if I want it. And I hear say Tompkins is all ready to take you back Monday. You stick to your books, man! You'll like it better being a doctor than mopping floors."

They laughed loudly, not because what Howie had said

was funny, but because they were so glad to have him back. All the while Robby was thinking that if Fayette opened Monday morning, the ordeal was going to begin again—but he was ready.

CHAPTER TWENTY-ONE

T
HE RAIN that broke the heat spell began in the middle of the night. It came suddenly in a chill, windy deluge that hit sharply on tin roofs, thudded on wooden shingles, and struck windowpanes with the sound of dry peas. The rain fell in torrents into the widening pools of water along Main Street, where it could not run off fast enough into overloaded drains. Again and again, long stabs of lightning crossed the dark sky, the thunder following angrily.

The wild rain heightened Nellie Drake's alarm as she tossed sleeplessly in her bed, thinking of her husband locked in an iron-barred cell in Knoxville. The wakeful night was cruel and menacing. She wept helplessly into her pillow because Tom, a white man, was being punished for standing up against niggers. Her crying became even more anguished at the thought that her husband was punished for doing his patriotic duty to safeguard the honor of his two girls and all white Southern womanhood. It was because there weren't enough men like Tom that the world was being turned upside down, with black men lording it over the others. Ben Collins' warning had become true in a hurry.

Mrs. Drake's sleeplessness turned the night into agony. The rain was unceasing, and with each new gust of wind, unfamiliar noises pulled at doors and windows. Panic gripped her as she imagined a black man peering through slits in the window curtains and heard the fingering of a doorknob, followed by the slow prowl of someone groping for an opening into her unprotected home. The fear was beyond endurance, but she could only lie paralyzed in her bed, waiting for the menace to strike.

Her imaginary terrors did not end until the first glimmer of daylight crept in at the still rain-drenched windows. It was five o'clock then, and Mrs. Drake ran into the girls' room to awaken them for their first visit to their father since his arrest.

Arlene and Jenny still had sleep in their eyes after they were washed and dressed. With little appetite, they ate their breakfast of scrambled eggs and limp bacon, and drank hot coffee. Mrs. Drake made up sandwiches and cut a large slice of her husband's favorite molasses cake. She wrapped everything in wax paper and stuffed it into a brown grocery bag. It was still raining heavily when they were ready to leave.

They locked up the house and got into the car.

Mrs. Drake took the wheel, and the two girls sat beside her on the front seat. In silence, they drove slowly down the alternate road until they reached the four-lane highway. The wet asphalt stretched empty before them and melted into a cottony screen of falling rain on the horizon. The car went at a steady fifty-mile clip for nearly half an hour before they met the first blurred, yellow headlights piercing the gloom. The light stirred Arlene and Jenny out of their drowsiness. As the approaching glow grew brighter, the outline of a giant vehicle rose into view. When it came closer, the huge form began to take shape. Soon they could see that it was an Army tank, its long gun pointing straight at them.

The girls sat up stiffly as Mrs. Drake screamed, "Lord save us! It's the Army!" Although her hands pressed tightly on the steering wheel, the car slowed down to a crawl. Until now, she had refused to believe that Washington would dare send armed men into Jameson. But they were here, sent to humiliate and punish brave Southerners. Wide-eyed, she watched the tank's approach and heard the thunderous clattering of its metal treads. Incredulously she counted seven of them as they followed each other inexorably in a slow-moving column; their roar becoming louder all the time. The tanks were followed by invading canvas-topped jeeps in which she caught a shadowy glimpse of helmeted men wearing waterproofs. The trucks came last, with their olive-drab canvas flapping in the wind like the loose garment of some monstrous figures.

"Oh, Mom!" wailed Arlene. "What's going to happen

216

now? What will they do to Harry and Dad?" She began to sob loudly, while Jenny added her frightened whimpering.

Their mother pressed hard on the gas, as if in answer to the girl's outcry. With a jarring lurch, the car picked up speed. Only when they had left the military column well behind did she speak.

"Nothing is going to happen to Dad and Harry," she said sharply. "Stop your noise both of you! You two ain't never going back to school as long as those niggers are in there. You're old enough to do without schooling. You'll be getting married soon anyway."

The thought of Harry confined in a jail cell, so far removed from any church altar, made Arlene's sobbing louder and more convulsive. Her mother screamed at her with sudden energy.

"Stop that yowling! I've decided we're going to quit Jameson forever. As soon as your Dad comes home, we'll move near your Uncle Jim in Mississippi where a white girl is still safe."

Jenny, who did not have a steady boy friend, found the news promising. "They can't make us go to school with niggers where Uncle Jim lives," she agreed defiantly through her tears.

"They can't!" echoed Mrs. Drake. "Never!"

CHAPTER TWENTY-TWO

T
HE MILITARY COLUMN came to a halt at 7 a.m. sharp, after it had ringed Courthouse Square with tanks, machine guns, ammunition supplies, trucks, jeeps, two ambulances, and field kitchens. Five hundred tired-looking soldiers left their trucks, carrying rifles, to line up for briefing. Miraculously, the rain stopped, and the sun came out as the cooks prepared to serve breakfast.

News of the Army's arrival spread rapidly, and Main Street began to fill with churchgoers who stared unbelievingly but were forced to accept what their eyes and ears could not deny. The military address system sent out a wide-ranging message.

"We've got a job to do," boomed the amplified voice of the lieutenant in command, a West Pointer. "We're going to do it, regardless of what it takes." The curt words fell upon the gaping crowd like blows as the orders were repeated: "Keep moving! Keep going!"

No civilian traffic was in sight. The Army turned back all cars trying to enter the town and rerouted highway vehicles miles out of Jameson. The pedestrians stared nervously at the faces of the helmeted, young-looking troops and kept moving slowly in a steady stream toward Chestnut street. The crowd grew until it overflowed the sidewalks into the macadam road, edging its way toward Matthew Logan's church in Crestwood.

Joel Saunders was one of the crowd, but managed to keep at a snail's pace, staring awestruck at the military display. Its presence made the familiar street seem like alien territory, and the strangeness of it sent a queer sensation down his spine. The tank guns with their long dark muzzles were real, and he marveled how different this was from looking at movie or TV guns. He tried to imagine one of them blasting off in Main Street, but the fantasy just would not jell.

He remembered the first Junior White Crusade meeting at the Abbotts', and it was difficult to believe that all this started only a week ago. He was lucky, he thought, not to have been sucked very far into Harry Nelson's gang; those kids who waved Rebel flags at football games and cranked up a pride in the Confederacy were not just having fun; it was for real! It led to this shame of being invaded by soldiers carrying rifles with fixed bayonets.

Joel was swept along with the crowd until he reached Reverend Logan's church. A truck with television equipment was parked at the entrance. It reminded him of Collins' boast that he was putting Jameson on the map. He had made that promise good with a bang! Arnold's Hotel was filled to bursting with reporters who were sending out the ugly story of Fayette High to every part of the globe.

On the sidewalk, a man spoke into a microphone held before his lips by a TV reporter, and Joel elbowed his way to them.

"Our big mistake in this town," said the man into the mike, "was to let only a few people carry the ball for law and order. That's how Collins got the idea that he was so strong around here. Now we've got to show the White Crusade crowd how things really stand! I'm not a member of this church but I came out of respect. . . ."

The interviewer cut him off politely and moved to a woman standing with her husband and teen-age son and daughter at her side. Joel stayed near the reporter and heard him ask, "Ma'am, what do you think of the attack on Reverend Logan?"

The woman was shy and began in a shaky voice, "It's a punishment on all of us, because we have two kinds of law here. One for colored and one for white. That makes everybody have disrespect for the law. It's time we realized the truth. We must all take the blame for what happened to our pastor. We kept our boy and girl out of school, because we were afraid of what some neighbors would say, or an accident, or something like that. But they're going back tomorrow when Fayette opens." Her husband nodded agreement.

220

Joel caught sight of Mrs. Barlow and her family and followed at their heels into the church, but he lost them as they hurried to their pew.

There were lights and cameras rigged up inside. The overflow crowd came prepared to hear Reverend Logan's sermon delivered by a substitute; they filled the seats rapidly and stood along the walls. William Cobb and his wife were present—the principal of Fayette looked visibly distressed, his face a mirror of his inner struggle between sympathy for his injured friend and unbending disapproval of Logan's radical views.

The lights were focused on Mr. Hayworth, the youngest of the church trustees, who took the minister's pulpit. Near him, in the full glare of television illumination sat the undistinguished-looking George Brown, who overnight had become known to nearly everyone in town as "the other man who walked with the colored kids."

The trustee began the service with a benediction; then came the reading of telegrams and cables for Matthew Logan, sent by well-wishers from all over the world. The sermon itself was long, and Hayworth read very slowly, with great solemnity to the hushed listeners.

In it the absent minister bared his soul to the public and took upon himself the heaviest share of blame for the Jameson crisis.

The sermon indicted the entire white community for its denial to the Negro of equal education and equal opportunity for economic improvement, documenting the charges carefully. The minister accused himself and the townspeople of distorting their religion because of the sinful wish to retain whatever privileges of pride and material power that was still left to them as the evil heritage of slavery.

"To have a docile beast of burden," Mr. Hayworth read, "you must have a degraded one."

Logan reviewed the town's efforts to circumvent the Supreme Court order and his own failure to come out honestly and courageously for the moral right of colored children to be in Fayette High School.

"I remained silent," he confessed, "and my sin was the gravest of anyone in Jameson. Nor did I protest the oppressive conditions we white people impose on our Negro brothers. I remained silent though I knew that a black man can be scorned and maltreated with impunity by the most depraved, so long as he has a white skin."

The final words which Hayworth read had the ring of prophecy, and the trustee delivered them with deep emotion.

"Law and order and moral health are one and the same thing. To be lasting, it must come from one's own conscience; there is no other force that can for long protect our homes, our churches, and our schools against chaos."

With those words the sermon ended, and the crowd silently made its way out of the church.

CHAPTER TWENTY-THREE

Breakfast was over on Sunday morning when Robby shyly told his mother, "I'm not going to church with you, Mom. I've got to go into town. I want to visit Reverend Logan at the hospital."

"He will be pleased to see you!" she said, toning down the happiness which his announcement gave her and pretending that it was a simple thing which he had decided to do this morning.

But she knew that he had just reached a great milestone in his life. His words were proof that he had come out of the week's suffering with something positive that would help him for the rest of his life. His decision to visit the white man told her that Robby had overcome some of the scourge of fear and

223

hatred within him; and out of his suffering, he had built a bridge (frail as it was) between himself and all men, whether black or white. He had reached safe ground and would grow up to a good manhood, for there was room in his heart for pity and for love. Robby was saved from the terrible loneliness of a man who could only hate, and Louella Jones gave silent thanks to her Creator for this priceless gift given to her son.

Robby rushed off with long steps, half-running to reach Linda Tilson before she went to church. He found her still at home, wearing a starched pink cotton dress and high-heeled white shoes. He stared at her in amazement for a long time, as though he had forgotten how pretty she was.

"You sure look fine," he said, almost with a sigh, so sharp was his pleasure. "I didn't know you were so tall."

Linda's heart fluttered as she accepted the admiration in his eyes. Her joy was mingled with pride that handsome Robert Jones had come to take her to church this morning.

"You'll never guess why I'm here," he blurted out, remembering the purpose of his visit. "Let us go see Reverend Logan at the *hospital*. The two of us can call it a committee. We'll tell him how sorry we feel for what happened to him. If we go now there won't be a lot of people around, and he might be glad to see us."

This was not the same as going to church, where everyone in Mount Olive could see them together; but if Robby had asked Linda to walk with him on her high heels as far as Knoxville at this moment, she would have made a try. She did not need to be told that it was easier for him to chop a cord of firewood than enter the forbidden territory of Phelps Hospital to visit a white man. Linda was no less uncomfortable at the prospect, but it was enough that he had proposed it, for her to follow.

They walked down the steep dirt road leading into Main Street. Linda's heels wobbled over the small stones as she kept up with Robby's steady, long steps. "I wanted to look at the soldiers," she confided with excitement. "Now we can see everything on the way to Phelps."

As they walked by the neutral-looking faces of the military patrol, Robby gazed with grave eyes at the display of their sharp bayonets. Main Street seemed to him like a battlefield upon which a lull in the fighting had settled. He tried hard to believe now that the white soldiers were here to protect him, for it would be the beginning of jubilee if those guns and tanks were sent here by the President of the United States to back up *his* rights! Robby tingled at the thought. All at once he was acutely reminded that only a short while ago he had thought of running away. It was hard for him to understand that panic now. He wished he could talk to Linda about it, but did not know how to begin.

When they reached the hospital, they both stopped to stare at the clean white door with its high fanlight. Somewhere there was another entrance marked for colored help, but Robby decided not to look for it. He led the way up the wide stairs and held the door open for Linda. She went in bravely.

An elderly man at the reception desk looked up with a surprised frown. At Robby's polite request for permission to visit Reverend Logan, the disapproval did not go away, but the man said with a flicker of recognition, "You're the high school kids. Walk up those steps to the left. You'll find him on the floor above in Room Twelve. You know you're not supposed to come in through that door."

On the second floor, a colored man was mopping the floor in the hall. He stopped short when he saw them and pointed to a door. "I guess you want to see Reverend Logan," he said eagerly. "It's open. He's feeling fine this morning."

They found the minister looking out of the tall, old-fashioned window which reached high toward the ceiling. When he turned around, they saw that one side of his drawn face was heavily swathed with bandages. The uncovered eye seemed bright with pleasure.

"I am very glad you came," he said, greeting them as friends whom he had been expecting.

The bandage drew Robby hypnotically. He thought of the empty socket which it covered and became tongue-tied; the smooth phrases he had prepared seemed shabby and worthless at this moment.

The minister came to his aid, his lips curving into the resemblance of a smile. "I've been watching the soldiers from this window all morning," he said, and there was a faint feeling of triumph in his voice. "I have an idea we are not going to have quite as much trouble any more about your school days at Fayette."

He drew two chairs close to his own, explaining that his voice was not very strong. "I know you want to be a doctor, Jones," he said, whittling away at his visitors' shyness. "But what about you, miss; what are your plans for the future?"

"I am going to be a history teacher," Linda answered primly.

"That's good!" Logan exclaimed. "A fine teacher is heaven's best gift to our country. Here I am, already up and about, thanks to some excellent men who teach medicine." His single eye turned on Robby. "We can use a lot of new doctors!"

Robby Jones was silent, thinking that there wasn't one colored physician or nurse in all of Jameson. Suddenly he felt as if his private thoughts were a reproach to the sick man, and he smiled with embarrassment.

Reverend Logan pointed to a sheet of paper lying on the small table near his bed. "Over there are the notes I have been working on for our weekly church bulletin," he said. "I want to take advantage of your being here. Will you do me the favor of bringing it to Reverend Wilkins? We have plans to talk it over. You can both read it. It is a pledge which is to be presented to our church members. Please tell your pastor that I am expecting another visit from him soon. We have a great deal to talk about.

Robby and Linda listened transfixed, as the minister went on to reveal his plan for a special Sunday School class for Negro and white children meeting together in his church. They forgot he was not well and therefore tired easily. When the nurse came to say they had to go, there was no time left for

Robby to tell him why they had come to see him. But it no longer mattered, for he knew this white man could understand such things without being told.

Logan held them a moment longer. "Be sure both of you read that pledge before you deliver it," he said earnestly. "Not many people in town can live up to it at this time, not even if they promise to do so. But for some, nothing less will be enough. It will take perseverance to make it work, but we won't be discouraged, will we?" He smiled a wan good-bye. "Thank you for coming to see me."

As soon as they reached the street, Robby came to a sudden stop. "I've got to read that thing right now," he said, leading the way around the corner of the building. When he found a spot where they would not be disturbed, he propped himself against the brick wall and held the sheet that was covered with fine script close to his chest. He read the first long sentence to himself, oblivious of Linda's impatience.

"Wow!" he exclaimed, and began to read to her.

I pledge to live in Christian brotherhood: To recognize that the rights and privileges granted to Americans in our country belong equally to all citizens, regardless of race, color, or creed. Among these rights must be included equal opportunity for jobs, education, housing, the right to vote and to serve on juries, the right to use all public facilities, including . . .

Robby could not go on without commenting on the incredible words. "That man sure didn't leave out a thing! He means restaurants and movies and buses and drinking fountains! Listen to this." He went on reading.

228

I will strive to conquer all prejudice against our Negro citizens and to eliminate all terms of reference which are defamatory in nature which are the result of prejudice and in turn give nourishment to the evil practice.

When he had finished reading the entire pledge, Robby covered his face with the sheet of paper as if to shut out everything else. A moment later, when his brown eyes looked into Linda's he sighed deeply. "It sure would be a hallelujah day when they get ready to do all that. You can wake me up when the time comes."

On the way home, Robby's need to have his thoughts tidy and in order—ready for tomorrow's return to school— made the urge to talk about Baker's visit compelling. He had to know the truth about himself, even if it meant confessing how close he had been to running away.

"I've got to tell you something, Linda," he said, keeping his eyes straight ahead. "It's about Joyce Baker's father."

"Oh, that! I know about Friday night—the very next morning Mr. Baker started telling people you were leaving to go to school up North. But I didn't believe it. That man just doesn't know how to tell the truth."

It staggered Robby to realize that not only she, but most of Mount Olive knew all about Baker's offer.

"I didn't tell him I was going!" he cried in sudden outrage. A moment later he added quietly, "Baker is a liar, but I'm not telling the whole truth either. In my mind, I sure enough wanted to run away. Maybe if Mom hadn't told him to wait for an answer, I would have taken up that offer right away." He mustered the courage to look sideways at Linda, and then he went on, "That was the night I was positive they wouldn't let us go back to Fayette after they hurt Logan. I started to run inside of me, even before Baker came to our house. He just made it worse."

Like quicksilver, the moodiness with which he had begun the confession lifted. The idea that Baker's offer could be a magic wand to provide him with an education struck him as ridiculous. He shook his head in silent disbelief that he could have been foolish enough to fall for it, even for a minute.

"It's just the way Howie said," Robby continued, as though Linda had the power to divine what had gone through his mind. "There's no place to run. No place, anywhere in the U.S.A., where they hand you the keys to the city. And you know what? I've just decided that we've got to do something about Jerry. I've got to see him; maybe with Howie, and make him come back to Fayette."

When they were on their own road, climbing slowly up the hill, Linda felt Robby's hand closing over hers. Her heart skipped, and her cheeks grew hot as she realized that he was holding her hand in broad daylight.

Robby suddenly began to chuckle. "You want to know something, girl; I've decided to move my Knoxville office right into the Medical Building in Jameson. No colored-town shack for this doc. I'll be the first black doc on Main Street." He enjoyed talking about it, even as a joke, for some day, in the distant future, a colored man would make it. For sure. The chuckle became uproarious laughter. "I just remembered I still got to graduate from high school and get into college and then into a medical school and graduate again." He stopped in his tracks. "I wonder what it's going to be like tomorrow," he added, still laughing. "There might be soldiers right inside the school."

"I hate Mr. Simon Baker," said Linda, ignoring his levity. "He had no right to tell people you were going away when it wasn't true. I guess your mother must have told you to wait with the answer because she knew you wouldn't swallow his talk if you had a chance to think it over."

Robby's eyes widened as the truth suddenly struck him. His mother and Howie and Reverend Wilkins and the lawyer from the NAACP had it all fixed to keep right on trying, even if Fayette stayed closed on Monday. They would have helped him stick with it and would have found some way of keeping up the fight.

Linda felt the firm pressure of Robby's hand and smiled. She wished Joyce Baker were around to see—the thought came and went at quickly as a bird in flight, gone before she was fully aware of it. Everyone was standing around in front of the church, and she was proud of being seen walking hand in hand with Robby. It was happiness just to feel that she had been able to help him a little during this week of trouble.

CHAPTER TWENTY-FOUR

J OEL SAUNDERS waited at the doors of Fayette High early Monday morning. At this hour, students drifted in slowly, and he was impatient for Robby's arrival. There were no hostile pickets today. The alien Army troops standing guard gave him the heebie-jeebies. One minute he felt like a defender of his school, ranged on the side of the bayonet-carrying soldiers. But the next minute the presence of the troops made him angry. He hated standing around, but he had made a vow to himself that he would show Jones he was sorry for the rotten reception of last Monday.

The Negroes soon appeared with Jerry Moore restored to their ranks. Today Robby led the way slowly toward the entrance, looking around him with the feeling of having the freedom to examine the school building just as if he were seeing it for the very first time. He was more certain than ever now of his right to be there even though he knew that he was not yet truly a part of the school.

He knew at once why Joel was standing in his path. When they were face-to-face Robby said, "Hi, Saunders!"

"Hi, Jones!" came the answer, the way they used to exchange greetings when they met by accident on Main Street. Robby felt as though he had suddenly lost a bad week-old toothache. They were not friends any more, but neither were they enemies.

In the assembly hall the curtains opened, and Mr. Cobb appeared on the stage. A single handclap set off a thin round of applause, but before it had time to die, the air was punctuated by a loud, dissenting "Boo!" Fresh applause broke out in force; it was the answer to the heckler, and it became louder, reinforced by loud whistling and stamping of feet.

Clearly it was a demonstration of the students' loyalty to the principal, but he held up his hand for order. His face was expressionless despite the show of support. He gave the signal to stand, and they sang "The Star-Spangled Banner." When the pledge of allegiance was over, Mr. Cobb introduced a stranger, Mr. James Danbury, the County Attorney.

"I am here in my official capacity," he announced in clipped speech. "I have come to tell you how you must act as long as you are students in this school. I cannot tell you how you must think, or what to believe, but I am empowered to tell you how you will be expected to behave."

233

He declared that he would read to them the complete text of the federal restraining order issued on Friday afternoon by Judge Payne of Knoxville.

"What you are going to hear is an injunction," he said, "prohibiting interference in any way with the legal right of the Negro students to attend this school. It is enforceable—for minors as well as adults, whether you are inside or outside this building. But first I want to remind you of some of the details this document covers—just in case someone here does not know, or has forgotten what has been going on here."

He then recited the acts of torment inflicted on the Negro students. The assembly heard out the ugly facts in embarrassed silence; some learning the harsh truth for the first time.

"They have been jostled," he said, "spat on, tripped in classrooms, threatened with knives, manhandled, and have been the butt of filthy language. . . ."

He kept the obscenity perpetrated on Joyce Baker for the very last, using it as a sharp goad to their conscience.

"A colored girl has had her head doused in a commode—that's a toilet bowl, for those of you who are unfamiliar with that fancy word. It took half a dozen brave Fayette students, girls and boys, to do this to their victim."

The speaker permitted the gasp of shock to make itself heard before he continued, "The ugly record is much longer, but I think I have made clear what this federal injunction demands of you. All cases of its violation will be turned over to the Justice Department in Washington. But the school board will support a faculty recommendation to expel students guilty of its breach even before the Justice Department acts.

"I doubt very much if ever before in American history has there been an instance in which a federal injunction was read to guide the conduct of high school students. This is a most unpleasant task for all of us—except, of course, for a vicious few in your midst. My final word of warning is that this injunction applies to the use of any sort of pressure against the Negroes—direct or indirect."

Fayette's unsavory contribution to U.S.A. school history was painfully clear as the reading ended. There were confused, scattered handclaps as though applause was in doubtful taste.

Mr. Cobb took Mr. Danbury's place and showed no inclination to clear the atmosphere. "I have this to add to the official statement," he declared. "It costs ten thousand dollars a day to keep the Army in Jameson. We could use that money for projects urgently needed here; on scholarships, for example. But the troops will remain until the lawless elements are convinced that we will not tolerate mob rule. Let us hope this will not take too long to bring about so that we can return to normal life. We can't afford to lose any more time this term."

Cobb's voice had suddenly become less harsh as he added, "A word must be said for the good behavior of the Negro students. We take note especially of Robert Jones who, because he was the leader of this group, became the target. . . ."

The sentence was left unfinished by the outburst of applause, and the principal waited patiently, smiling for the first time this morning.

"We have received many letters of praise for the colored students from all parts of the world——"

Wild applause interrupted him, but he stood smiling and holding up a sheaf of telegrams. Robby and Linda, sitting side-by-side, exchanged shy looks.

When the assembly was over, a senior sat down at the piano to play "Roll Out the Barrel," which the principal favored as an exit march. The students filed into the aisles singing lustily. Robby sang, too, almost as energetically as the white students.

That evening, without prearrangement, the seven met in front of the A.M.E. Zion Church. Linda brought a letter. Waving it in front of them, she said, "It's from Joyce Baker. She feels bad about being away from us. She's coming home for the Christmas holiday and wants to know if you're angry at her."

"Who dat?" Robby joked.

"Aren't you sorry for her?" Linda demanded.

Robby seemed deep in thought before he answered, "I'm not angry at her, but she should have stayed right here, if she didn't want to feel bad. The kids that messed her up were dirty. She was clean; she should have stayed."

Linda nodded. It was easy for her now to feel sorry for Joyce who was so far away. She was even sorrier for the elegant Mrs. Baker.

"If they did it to me," she said, "I would have been too mad to run away, and I wouldn't have tried to hide what they did." She clenched her hands into tight fists, crumpling Joyce's letter. "I'd tell everybody! To make more people mad!"

The open space in front of the church was filling with the entire junior population of Mount Olive. All the small fry came with their older brothers and sisters. They were drawn to the spot like bees to a honeycomb, because it was good to be together in victory. Everyone could bask in the glory that hung over the seven like a halo.

Round-eyed Pete McDonald asked, "Is it the truth—you Fayette kids got telegrams from all over?"

"The God's honest truth," Jerry shouted.

"Yeah! Yeah!" the small fry chorused.

The feeling of victory was infectious. Robby felt good. Not Pete, nor anybody else, could spoil it for him—nobody had to tell him that the day of jubilee was not coming as easily as it sounded, but it was coming!

It was dark when Howie and Reverend Wilkins appeared. The young people made room for them on the church steps. The old man sighed with pleasure as he sat down and made himself comfortable. He looked at the upturned faces of the children, knowing that they were waiting for him to place a suitable crown on this special day, and he smiled happily.

He put an affectionate hand on Howie's shoulder as he said, "You know, Howard Carter is up on a lot of things. He just told me on the way over here that three-fifths of the people in the world are colored. If that's true, then God must really love colored people to make so many of them." He laughed softly, not a bit proud to borrow from Lincoln's words about the common people.

"But all people are the same," the pastor added to rein in too much pride. "It isn't color and it isn't blood that makes people act in a certain way. It is how they have been taught and what they believe."

He smiled broadly. "Take Joshua. He was a strong man and his army was big, but all that strength wasn't enough for knocking down those Jericho walls. Yet he won. All he did was to make a long blast on a ram's horn, but when his people heard that trumpet, they all gave a great shout, and it was enough to make them free. They acted that way because they *believed* in the righteousness of their cause. Their belief turned the shout into a roar that was like all the mountains in the world breaking apart, sending rocks and boulders crashing. It was that great shout which made the walls of Jericho fall as flat as bread without yeast. That's how Joshua's people were able to go up into that City of Jericho—every last man of them."

Robby's eyes were shining when Jacob Wilkins finished his story. Linda was at his side, and their fingers locked. He knew that getting into Fayette was only the beginning. The couplet sang itself in his mind:

> *I thought I heard them say*
> *There were lions in the way. . . .*